"I think we shou ... our next date." She briefly closed her eyes. "I mean *meeting*. We can save that story for our next meeting." Kiara stood abruptly. "I think it's time for me to go."

"Okay," Trey said with a laugh. "I'll walk you out."

They made their way down the spiral stairs.

"I had a nice time tonight," Kiara said when she reached the door. She turned around to find him watching her intently.

"I had a nice time, as well." Trey took a step closer to her. "I enjoyed getting to know you a little better." He was so close, Kiara was afraid to breathe.

"Me, too," she whispered. His eyes dropped to her lips. She forced herself to swallow the lump in her throat.

When his hand reached up to cup her face, Kiara completely froze. *There's no way he's going to kiss me, right? We just met each other.*

"Do you want me to stop?" he asked.

Say yes. Say yes. Say yes. "No," she said, moments before his lips came crashing down onto hers.

Dear Reader,

I was excited for the chance to write another novel in the Millionaire Moguls series, and writing about Trey Moore and Kiara Woods did not disappoint. Since I often write connecting stories, writing Trey and Kiara's story gave me the opportunity to write about characters who hadn't met prior to the novel.

I hope you also enjoy catching up with Kyra Reed, from the Bare Sophistication series, who is close friends with Kiara in *A Los Angeles Passion*. In true Kyra fashion, she can't be anyone but herself.

Make sure you follow me to stay updated on my latest releases!

Much love,

Sherelle

authorsherellegreen@gmail.com

www.bit.ly/SherelleGreensCoffeeCorner

@SherelleGreen

A
LOS ANGELES
Passion

SHERELLE
GREEN

HARLEQUIN® KIMANI™ ROMANCE

Special thanks and acknowledgment are given to Sherelle Green
for her contribution to the Millionaire Moguls series.

Recycling programs
for this product may
not exist in your area.

ISBN-13: 978-1-335-21687-8

A Los Angeles Passion

Printed in U.S.A.

⊕ HARLEQUIN®
™ www.Harlequin.com

Sherelle Green is a Chicago native with a dynamic imagination and a passion for reading and writing. She enjoys composing emotionally driven stories that are steamy, edgy and touch on real-life issues. Her overall goal is to create relatable and fierce heroines who are flawed, just like the strong and sexy heroes who fight so hard to win their hearts. There's no such thing as a perfect person…but when you find that person who is perfect for you, the possibilities are endless. Nothing satisfies her more than writing stories filled with compelling love affairs, multifaceted characters and intriguing relationships.

Books by Sherelle Green

Harlequin Kimani Romance

A Tempting Proposal
If Only for Tonight
Red Velvet Kisses
Beautiful Surrender
Enticing Winter
Wrapped in Red (with Nana Malone)
Falling for Autumn
Waiting for Summer
Nights of Fantasy
A Miami Affair
Her Unexpected Valentine
A Los Angeles Passion

Visit the Author Profile Page
at Harlequin.com for more titles.

To my in-laws, Bernadine and Isaiah,
for all your support and encouragement.
I feel so lucky and blessed to have each of you in my life.
Mom, ever since my first book event, you have always
attended and supported me. Not only am I grateful
to have you present at these events, but other authors
and readers alike love your enthusiasm and always look
forward to seeing you. Together, we always have a good
time and our closeness means the world to me. Dad, the
fact that you've shown an interest in my work and have
pushed to help me take my career even further truly
warms my heart. You keep me laughing and you already
know I'm always down to hear one of your stories.

Not only am I grateful to have an amazing husband,
but I feel blessed to have such kindhearted,
supportive and loving in-laws.

Chapter 1

Trey Moore could barely conceal his anticipation as he ran his long fingers over the smooth, creamy piece of his latest obsession.

"That's it," he whispered, pinching at a couple of curled edges that were beautifully laid out on the table before him. "Come to me, baby."

For months, he'd been preparing for this very moment. Trey reached for his scotch on the rocks before sitting on the high chair of his dining room table. He took a measured sip of the cool liquid and observed the printed cream-colored pages of his screenplay, which was currently divided into scenes.

Trey had been cooped up in his Brentwood, LA, estate for nearly seventy-two complete hours, and he was no closer to being finished with his latest screenplay than he was before he'd taken his hiatus.

For Trey, there was nothing more frustrating than having writer's block when his agent and producers were on his back for the next Hollywood hit. He'd known, the minute he'd accepted this job, that he'd run into a few issues toward the end. He prided himself on only agreeing to write screenplays for stories that he truly believed were special in their own way. However, even he'd admit that, initially, he hadn't seen the producer's vision behind this particular project. As time grew and he let the story line foster in his head a bit, he'd begun to change his mind.

Every time Trey wrote a screenplay, he invariably got that feeling in the pit of his stomach that he'd figure out how to tie up every loose end in the story finally. Call it writer's intuition or good old-fashioned luck, he always knew instinctively that he'd be able to finish things satisfactorily, and just an hour ago, he'd gotten that hunch again.

The feeling had come a little later than he'd liked, but luckily, he still had a couple of weeks to pull perfection from the last few scenes he'd written down in an effort to appease his agent and producers. It was mid-September and he hadn't promised them anything final until mid-October.

Taking another sip of his scotch, he picked up one of the action scenes and read his handwritten sticky notes plastered across the paper. "Come on, Trey," he said, closing his eyes. "What's missing here?"

He kept his eyes closed as he imagined the scene

playing out in his mind as it would in the movie. He was only partially into his vision when he heard keys jingling in his front door. Trey opened his eyes and glanced down at his rose gold watch.

"Carmen," he said aloud as he shook his head and headed toward his front door. There was only one person who could be coming into his home at eleven o'clock at night.

"What do you want?" he said, crossing his arms over his chest the moment the door peeked open.

"Dang, big bro. Is that any way to greet your favorite sister?"

"You're my only sister."

"Precisely the reason you should be more grateful to see me."

"You're right," he said with a laugh as he reached for the car seat that held his nephew, Matthew. "Hey, M-dog," he said as he picked up the six-month-old. "How's my boy doing?"

"Ugh." Carmen frowned. "Why do you insist on calling him M-dog?"

"Because it's way better than you and Mom insisting on calling him Matty. There's nothing manly about the nickname Matty. Are you trying to raise your son to permanently be in the friends zone with every girl he meets?"

"Shut up," Carmen said, lightly slapping Trey's shoulder. "M-dog isn't a good nickname, either. You're lucky I love you because had anyone else called him that, I would have nipped it in the bud right away."

Trey smiled, knowing she meant it. Although Trey

and Carmen didn't have the same father, they were extremely close. Trey's stepdad—who was also Carmen's father—had been around for most of his life, and since Trey's relationship with his own father was strained, he appreciated his stepfather.

Through his biological dad, Reginald Moore, Trey also had two half brothers, Derek and Max. Since they all had different mothers, they hadn't been too close growing up. Like him, Derek also had an uneasy relationship with their father. Actually, Derek's relationship with Reginald was much worse than Trey's. Max was the only son who was close to Reginald, because he'd had the benefit of growing up with Reginald in his life and always had him around.

"Have any scotch?" Carmen stepped away from the foyer and walked into the kitchen area that was connected to the dining room and living room.

"You already know I do." Trey handed baby Matthew back to his sister as he pulled out a glass to pour scotch. "I thought you weren't drinking any liquor, though? When did that change?"

"Oh, it didn't," Carmen said with a sneaky smile. "The scotch is for you."

Trey stopped midpour. "For me? I already have a glass I was sipping on before you arrived."

"Great. Then maybe you should get that glass."

Trey leaned against the counter. "Enough stalling, Carmen. I'm happy to see you and my nephew, but why are you here?"

Carmen nuzzled her nose with Matthew's tiny button before speaking. "Well, as you know, Max has been trying to get me a few gigs, but even with his connections as my talent agent, I haven't gotten a lot of bites."

Trey nodded, well aware of Carmen's frustration with her acting career. His sister was talented, and seeing that their mom was a famous actress in her day, Hollywood expected that at least one of her children would follow her path. Surprisingly, Trey had found his niche in LA as a prominent screenplay writer. However, Carmen was still trying to emulate their mother. Trey knew that all she needed was a big break to showcase her talent, and he was hoping that Max, his half brother and Carmen's agent, could help her in any way possible.

"So, it looks like my hard work is finally paying off. I landed a minor role on a weekly television series."

"That's great, sis." Trey gave her a quick hug, careful not to crush Matthew. "I knew you'd get a break soon enough."

"I'm really excited," Carmen said, beaming from ear to ear. "I couldn't wait to tell you. I even wanted to tell Scott and gloat a little, but I don't want to jinx anything."

Scott was Carmen's ex and Matthew's father. Trey had always gotten along well with Scott, but Scott didn't support Carmen's dream of becoming a full-time actress, so the two had split right before Carmen found out she was pregnant. Trey was proud of his sister for not letting her dream of spending the rest of her life with Scott and raising a family together deter her from following her other goal of becoming an actress.

"I understand that." Trey playfully nudged her on

the head like he'd done since she was little. "When do you start filming?"

"Funny you should ask." Carmen perked up. "I've been informed that it will take two weeks to film the pilot episode and I'm needed on set starting tomorrow. Which brings me to the reason I'm here."

Trey squinted his eyes when Carmen glanced from him to Matthew, then back to him. "Oh, no, sis. You've got to be kidding me. You already know I've got this thing to finish. Hell, I haven't even been out the house in days."

"I know, Trey. And I wouldn't ask if I had other options. I need someone to watch Matthew for two weeks while I film."

"The full two weeks!" Trey didn't mean for his voice to carry, but just the thought of him babysitting a six-month-old while trying to make this tight deadline was enough to send him into a slight panic, and Trey was *not* the panicky type. "Are you sure I'm the best option?"

"Best? Probably not. Only? Absolutely. You already know that Mom and Dad are on their African safari. And Scott is traveling between New York and Miami throughout the rest of this month on business, so he's not even in LA. I would ask Scott's parents if they weren't in Germany for the next few weeks. And I can't get a two-week nanny on such short notice. I know the timing isn't ideal for you, but I could really use your help right now."

Carmen shot him her big-puppy-dog-eyes that usually did the trick when she was trying to convince him to do something he didn't want to do. Trey lifted Matthew's tiny hand in his.

"Carm, I've never watched a child on my own for that long, let alone an infant."

"You used to watch me when I was little and you're only eight years older than me."

Trey shook his head. "The first time I babysat you on my own, I was twelve and you were four. That's hardly an infant."

"Whatever." Carmen shrugged. "The point is, you did fine back then and I'm sure you'll do fine now. There will be other times you have to watch your nephew, so you might as well start now. Plus, I really need your help. I've been hoping to land a gig like this and it may just be the opening I've been waiting for."

Trey sighed. He really did want Carmen to go for her dreams and he knew firsthand that the set wasn't a good place for infants. He recalled a time when his stepdad had been out of town and the babysitter had gotten sick. So his mom had been forced to bring him and a colicky Carmen on set for a movie she was shooting. It hadn't been pretty.

His eyes landed back on Matthew's adorable brown face and chubby baby cheeks. "Okay," he said reluctantly. "I'll babysit M-dog for two weeks."

"Oh my God. Oh my God. Oh my God." Carmen kissed Trey's cheek before handing Matthew to him. "Thank you so much, big bro. I owe you big-time!"

"I plan on collecting, too," he said with a laugh. His joke fell on deaf ears because Carmen was already halfway to the front door. "Where are you going?"

"I'll be right back." Ten minutes later, Trey was sorry he'd asked. It took no time for his home to go from the ultimate bachelor pad to a nursery straight out of an HGTV show.

"Carm, what is all this stuff?"

"This," she said, waving her hands around everything she'd placed in his living room, "is everything you will need to turn Casa De Trey into Matty's Baby Manor."

Trey handed Matthew back to his sister as he tried not to freak out by all the paraphernalia scattered around. *Baby swing. Baby mat. Baby carrier. Baby bathtub. Blankets. Stuffed animals. Pop-up crib. Diapers. Bottles. Pacifiers.* His mind couldn't even comprehend all the stuff needed to care for an infant.

"What in the world is all this?" he asked as he pointed to a mound of what appeared to be pieces of some type of toy.

Carmen smiled. "That's Matty's ExerSaucer."

"His exer…what?"

"His ExerSaucer." Carmen pulled out her phone with her free hand to show him a picture of Matthew sitting in one. "It's like an activity center for babies. It helps keep him busy. I had to break it apart to get it in my car, but I figured you could put it back together."

"Damn, Carmen. You might as well have brought over your entire house."

"I tried," she said with a laugh. "Also, even though Matty is a baby, try to limit the cursing around him. You never know what types of things babies pick up at a young age. And I also have a large tote bag that has his formula in it with instructions on scoops and how much water to add. His medicine is in there, too, as well as his Baby Bullet."

Trey's eyes widened. "Baby bullet? Do I even want to know what that is?"

"It's what you will use to blend his baby food." Carmen searched the floor until her eyes landed on a bin of baby food. "This bin should have all the food needed to blend your own recipes. Nothing too fancy. Just sweet peas. Mashed bananas. Stuff like that. It's not enough for two weeks, but should be enough for a week. And it needs to be refrigerated."

Trey lifted the bin and walked to the kitchen to place it in the refrigerator. He'd only agreed about twenty minutes ago, and already, he had to remind himself why he was doing this. Carmen's phone rang, interrupting his thoughts.

"Oops, I forgot I had this call. I have to take this." She rushed to Trey and handed him Matthew. "I'm going to miss my baby boy. Mama loves you," she said to her son as she showered him with kisses before answering her phone.

"This is Carmen. Can you please hold for a moment?" She glanced at Trey. "Are you good? You know you can call me anytime. In the large tote, I also left detailed instructions on everything, so you should be okay. He's already been fed tonight and I just changed him before we arrived. Tonight should be easy since he pretty much sleeps through the night. I can't tell you how much I appreciate this."

Carmen was already out the door before Trey could

formulate a response. Once they were alone in his home, Trey glanced down at the wide-eyed baby in his arms, unsure if he should be more worried about babysitting Matthew or if Matthew should be worried about him being the babysitter.

"We'll get through this, right, M-dog?" In response, Matthew blew a couple of spit bubbles before scrunching his forehead. "What does that face mean?" Trey asked, observing his nephew a little closer. "Are you agreeing with me?"

Matthew gurgled some more bubbles before he spit up and let out a loud wail.

"Oh, hell," Trey yelled as the spit-up ran from Matthew's mouth down to Trey's hand. Acting fast, Trey grabbed one of the blankets Carmen had left and began wiping off the baby's face.

Several minutes later, Trey still couldn't get Matthew to stop bawling. "Could this night get any worse," he said between the wails. On cue, his iPhone rang, displaying the last name he expected to see. *Reginald Moore? What does he want?*

Trey answered on the fourth ring. "Hello, this is Trey."

"Trey, this is your father. I have both your brothers on the line as well."

Trey pulled back to look at his phone as if it were contagious. "Max and Derek both?"

Each of his brothers greeted him. Trey *rarely* talked to his father and both brothers, so if they were all on the line, it had to be important.

"Trey, is that a baby in the background?" Reginald

asked. Trey glanced down at Matthew, who was still crying.

"Yeah, I'm babysitting my nephew. Let me put you all on a brief hold." Acting quickly on his feet, Trey managed to configure the pop-up crib with one hand and carefully place Matthew in the middle of the crib. As soon as he popped the pacifier into his nephew's mouth, the crying stopped.

Thank goodness. Trey glanced back at his phone, which was still on hold. *One problem down. One more left.* He sat on his large plush armchair that was next to the crib before resuming the conversation. "Okay, I'm back. So, tell me...what's the purpose of this call?"

He tried to leave the bitterness out of his voice, but it had been a long few months, and a call with his father never ended well.

Reginald cleared his throat. "Now that I have all of you on the phone, there's something very important that I need your help with." There was a slight pause before Reginald continued. "I know I've made a lot of mistakes in my life, but I would never do anything to hurt Prescott George, and I definitely did not do anything to the San Diego chapter. Granted, it was hard for me to accept that they would be named chapter of the year, but I would never stoop so low as to sabotage them. I gave Prescott George more than twenty-five years of my life, and as I've stated before, someone framed me."

Trey squeezed the bridge of his nose as his father continued to voice his innocence. Prescott George— or the Millionaire Moguls, as they were informally known—was a prestigious, all-male national organization that was as powerful as it was discreet. Until six months ago, Reginald had been a respected board member of the LA chapter of Prescott George, where his sons were also members.

After an internal investigation that proved Reginald was guilty of trying to sabotage the Prescott George San Diego chapter to keep them from winning the annual award, Reginald had been kicked out of the organization.

Trey, along with his half brothers, was horrified by the accusations and embarrassed that their father would try to harm the chances of another chapter. All of Reginald's sons were subjected to an internal investigation to make sure they hadn't assisted Reginald in his activities. And even though all three of them were cleared, the damage to the Moore name had already been done.

"I never believed you could be guilty, Dad," Max said. "I agree with you. I think you were framed."

Trey huffed into the phone. *Innocent? I doubt it.*

"Max, thank you for believing me," Reginald said. "Trey. Derek. I assume your silence means you don't believe I'm innocent. Quite frankly, I didn't expect either of you to believe me, but my innocence isn't the only situation I need to discuss with my boys."

The endearment Reginald voiced was probably the first Trey had ever heard. *My boys?* Max was close to Reginald, so it wasn't strange to hear him refer to Max with affection. However, Trey couldn't recall a time when his father had ever addressed him or Derek in any sort of way that indicated he was proud to be their father.

"Haven't you involved us in your recent situations enough?" Trey asked, finally getting over the surprise of the call. "It wasn't enough for our character to be questioned because of this investigation, but now you suddenly decide you want to have a heart-to-heart with all your sons when you're at your lowest?"

"I agree," Derek said. "Our lives were turned upside down from your mistakes. I think I've heard enough on this phone call."

"Just hear me out." Reginald cleared his throat again. "It's a little over three months before Christmas, and although I know I'm decades too late, it's time for me to make amends. When the investigation was going on this past spring, after a while, I became too weak and tired to continue to protest my innocence. But now I can't imagine going into the New Year with this burden on my back."

"What are you saying?" Max asked. "Why now, Dad?"

"Because now is all I've got, son." Reginald sighed. "I've just been informed that I have stage four prostate cancer. The doctors don't think I will live past the New Year, and although I know my sons don't owe me anything, I'm innocent of these crimes I've been convicted of. Before I die, I'd love nothing more than to clear my name, and my hope is that my sons will help me do that and preserve the Moore legacy."

Trey sat upright in his chair. *What? He's dying?* In some ways, Trey had felt like Reginald Moore would live forever, if only to remind him that he hadn't had the benefit of growing up with a father. Reginald didn't make Trey's top-one-hundred list of favorite people in the world, but even he'd admit that he'd always imagined Reginald lingering somewhere close by, hoping to appear on the list one day.

"Wow," Trey whispered, unable to take the sudden silence that filled the line. It only took a few moments for him to feel like the breath had been sucked from his lungs. Being a screenplay writer, he loved several things about films, but one of his favorite parts of a movie was the element of surprise. It was a scene that was so perfectly written and directed you couldn't predict what would happen next. When a surprise scene was written well, even the film crew applauded after it was acted out.

Since he was a screenwriter, he was often the one who wrote the surprises, *not* the one who was surprised. Even though Trey prided himself on always being able to see what would come next, he hadn't been able to predict the direction of this phone call. Nor could he have foreseen the sudden ache he felt in his heart at the thought of losing a father he'd never even gotten the chance to truly know.

Chapter 2

"Please tell me that is not my old college roomie, because I haven't seen her in so long I almost forgot what she looks like," said twenty-eight-year-old Kiara Woods as she stood from the outdoor table at a chic restaurant to give her friend a hug.

Miranda Jensen Ellicott shook her head before returning her embrace. "Girl, stop. It hasn't been that long."

Kiara gave her the side-eye. "Yes, it has. I haven't seen you since you got married to Vaughn."

"I know," Miranda said with a smile. "The newlywed life is keeping me pretty busy these days."

"With a husband like that, I'm sure it is."

Miranda smiled even wider. "If it were up to Vaughn, he'd have me pregnant and barefoot before the month is over. Luckily for me, he understands the importance of my work right now."

Kiara nodded in agreement. "And how are things going with Vaughn?"

Miranda's eyes lit up. "Wonderfully. He's actually a couple of blocks away, taking care of some business. We drove into LA together, so I just walked here."

"Aren't you guys cute," Kiara teased. "Even riding together for meetings and whatnot so that you don't have to be away from each other for long."

Kiara laughed when Miranda didn't try to deny it. "Seriously, it's great to see you so happy. How are things at your luxury B and B?"

"Everything is wonderful," Miranda said as the waiter approached. "Fall and winter are always busy for the B and B, so I expect to be at full capacity throughout the rest of the year. I can't complain." They placed their lunch order before they resumed their conversation.

"What about you?" Miranda asked. "How are things?"

Kiara grinned as she thought about the preschool and day-care center that she owned. "I'm honestly so proud of how much LA Little Ones Daycare and Preschool has grown. It's amazing to see my vision turn into a reality."

"Kiara, it's not just a preschool and day-care center," Miranda said. "It's *the* Hollywood preschool and day-care center. It's the place where LA's rich and famous want to take their children. Hell, I'm already hoping that I can get bumped up your waiting list when Vaughn and I start popping babies. We'd drive to LA for a great center like yours."

Kiara laughed. "You already know I'd bump you up the list."

"I'm just saying. Back in college, you always talked about owning your own day care, but I don't even think that you considered it would grow this much. And after the few rough patches you had a couple of years ago, you needed your business to be a success."

The waiter returned with two glasses of water and a plate of sliced lemons. "Thanks, girl." Kiara squeezed a lemon slice into her water before taking a sip. She thought about the words that Miranda left unspoken. Kiara had accomplished a lot before the age of thirty, but one circumstance that she'd never wanted to be a part of her journey was becoming a divorcée.

Everything had been going so well for her during the early years of her marriage. She'd thought that her unlucky days in love were finally over when she'd met Jerry. Little had she known that after two short years of marriage, she'd be getting a divorce and saying farewell to the one man who had promised to love her forever.

Diving into work had been the perfect distraction, and as the articles about her in the media put it, Kiara and her day care had become an overnight success in the childcare business. She hadn't had time for love, and quite frankly, she hadn't felt like anything was really missing from her life at that time.

But you feel like it is now. She briefly sighed as that little voice crept inside her thoughts, reminding her that she had once been a happy newlywed, too. She'd once worn the same smile that Miranda was wearing right now. She had once seen her future bright and clear with the man she loved before it was all taken away when he suddenly asked for a divorce.

"When was the last time you went out?" Miranda asked, breaking her thoughts.

Kiara took another sip of her water. "I go out."

Miranda pinned her with a hard stare. "Let me repeat my question. When was the last time you went out?"

"I can't remember," Kiara said with a shrug. "Maybe last month?"

"Are you sure?"

"Hmm." Kiara thought about it some more. "Maybe two months ago. Or three. I can't really remember."

Miranda shook her head. "Friend, the last time you told me about you going out was when a couple of your employees convinced you to check out that new jazz lounge. And that was way more than three months ago."

Kiara rapidly blinked. "Oh my God, I think you're right! That's the last time I remember going out just for the sake of going out."

"That's sad," Miranda said with a laugh. "The Kiara I knew back in college would never miss a party or pass up an opportunity to go out."

Kiara downed the rest of her water, wishing it was something stiffer. "Girl, that was before being an adult happened."

Miranda shook her head. "More like it was before life happened. Being an adult doesn't mean you can't have fun. Trust me, I understand being all about the business, but you've got to have a little fun, too, or before you know it, your life would have passed you by and you'll be wondering when was the last time you stopped to truly live in the moment."

As their food arrived, Kiara contemplated her friend's words, immediately realizing that Miranda was right. "I do need to learn to live a little more," Kiara said after a few moments. "But I also plan on building a franchise, so my schedule is bound to get even crazier."

"Building a franchise is a great idea," Miranda said. "Just keep in mind that a busy schedule doesn't mean you have to neglect your social life."

"True," Kiara said, nodding.

Miranda's phone dinged, interrupting their conversation. She frowned as she read the text message.

"Is everything okay?"

"Yeah." Miranda shot a quick reply. "I'm just worried that Vaughn is taking on too much. You know how we always teased a couple of our girlfriends back in college who used to say their main goal was to marry a Millionaire Mogul?"

"Of course," Kiara said with a laugh. "And then you go ahead and marry a Prescott George member despite how much we teased them."

Kiara knew all about the Prescott George organization, also called the Millionaire Moguls. She respected what they did for the community, but she never did understand why some women made it their main goal to land an elite member. Her ex-husband had even wanted to be a member, but Prescott George was exclusive with their membership, so he hadn't stood a chance.

Miranda grinned. "I know. I still can't believe it, either." She took another bite of her fruit salad before speaking again. "Well, Vaughn has been really busy with his San Diego chapter, but now he's also helping the LA chapter get back on their feet."

"Why? What happened?"

Miranda sighed. "I really shouldn't be saying anything, but they were suspended for six months when one of the LA board members tried to sabotage San Diego being chosen as chapter of the year. The person responsible orchestrated several break-ins, hacking of computers and files, and even the vandalism of some of the property. It got pretty bad, but finally, they figured out the man behind everything was Reginald Moore, a high-ranking board member."

"Wow," Kiara said, shaking her head. "I didn't hear anything about this."

"That's not surprising. Prescott George didn't want the bad press, so the board and the national organization declined to press charges and instead expelled Reginald Moore and placed the LA chapter on a six-month suspension. And apparently, he put up quite a fuss about everything."

"Of course he did." Kiara rolled her eyes. "There's nothing more annoying than a person who does something wrong, yet feels entitled and above the law. I'm sure he got what he deserved, and if you ask me, it even sounds like he got off easy. So, how was Vaughn looped into helping the LA chapter?"

Miranda opened her mouth to speak, but was cut off.

"We're a brotherhood," a voice said behind Kiara. "I'd never turn down helping out another chapter." She

turned to see Vaughn Ellicott approaching their outdoor table.

"Well, if it isn't Miranda's new husband…in the
flesh." Kiara stood to hug Vaughn before he hugged
his wife and sat in an empty seat.

"It's good to see you again, Kiara," Vaughn said
with a handsome smile. "And I can answer your question more fully, since I'm sure my wife was dying to
give you all the dirty details." To this, Miranda gave
Vaughn a Chuck E. Cheese grin.

"I'm just helping them by supporting some of their
charity initiatives and community involvement. One
man's mistake doesn't mean the entire chapter has to
suffer."

"That's nice of you," Kiara said.

Vaughn shrugged. "It's what I do." He looked toward his wife. "Are you ready to go shopping, baby?"

"I think so." Miranda pulled cash out of her purse to
pay for her portion of the meal.

Kiara lifted an eyebrow. "Vaughn, what in the world
made you agree to go shopping with Miranda? She takes
forever to make up her mind."

Miranda rolled her eyes. "I don't take as long as a
certain brown-eyed friend of mine. Besides, I can't believe I forgot to tell you… Vaughn is jet-setting us away
for a while to Dubai for a long and much-needed vacation, so there are a few things we have to pick up first."

Kiara smiled. "That's wonderful, you guys. I'm sure
you'll have so much fun." *Goodness, I'd love for a man
to take me away on a romantic vacation.* Her eyes widened. *Where did that thought come from?* Kiara fidg-

eted in her chair. It was official. Being around Miranda and Vaughn was making her long for things she'd given up on over a year ago. She didn't need to date. She didn't love. All she needed was her business, and if there was anything she'd learned from her ex-husband and the man she fell for after her divorce, it was that love wasn't forever. She *had* to remember that.

"I have an idea," Vaughn said, breaking her thoughts. "You should come with Miranda and me tonight to the party we're having to celebrate the LA chapter being back on their feet."

Miranda clapped her hands together. "That's a great idea, Vaughn!"

"I don't know," Kiara said, shaking her head. "Isn't it an exclusive party? I'll probably feel out of place."

Miranda rolled her eyes. "Right, because you don't own one of the most exclusive day cares in the city."

"Your sarcasm isn't needed," Kiara said with a laugh.

"It will be fine," Vaughn said. "There will be plenty of friends, family and supporters of the organization there. I consider you a friend and Miranda considers you family."

Kiara glanced from Vaughn to Miranda, who both awaited her response. *Oh, come on, girl. You know you need a night out.* "Okay," Kiara said. "I'll come. If I'm being honest, I'll admit that I've been dying to get dressed up."

"So glad you're coming." Miranda winked at Kiara. "And you may even land a Millionaire Mogul of your own."

"Ha! You wish." Kiara planned on keeping the promise she made to herself to refrain from dating to focus on building her business and franchise. Besides, she was done with rich men. Been there. Done that. She doubted she'd even find a man who remotely kept her interest tonight.

Chapter 3

"Okay, so even I have to admit that this is pretty lavish for an all-male organization," Kiara whispered to Miranda. Kiara never considered herself someone who was easily impressed, but she was in awe of the luxurious twelfth-floor penthouse suite in the downtown Los Angeles Fine Arts Building that served as the home for the LA chapter of Prescott George. The place was huge and easily accommodated a few hundred people. Given that even some of the most upscale penthouse suites in LA were smaller than the norm in other cities, this was impressive.

"The Moguls never go cheap," Miranda whispered back. "Every party I attend with Vaughn is grander than the last."

The Moguls' motto, written on the wall, caught her

eye. *From generation to generation, lifting each other up.* She'd heard their motto before, but for some reason, seeing it written in an official Prescott George chapter location felt different.

Kiara followed close behind Miranda and Vaughn as they made their rounds and greeted other Moguls and their families, respectfully introducing her as a close family friend. Kiara wore her most professional smile and tried her best not to fidget under the stare of some of the Moguls.

"Could you pretend to be a little more comfortable?" Miranda teased.

Kiara frowned. "I can't help it. I almost feel as if I'm on display here."

"Well, you do look fabulous, my friend. But I'm sure it's because of the type of party this is, too. Some of the Moguls are trying to figure out if you're going to rent them."

Kiara lifted an eyebrow. "Rent them? Exactly what type of party is this?"

"Funny you should ask," Miranda said with a sneaky smile. Before Miranda could explain, Kiara was tapped on her shoulder.

"Well, if it isn't Kiara Woods of LA Little Ones." Kiara turned to glance over her shoulder and was pleasantly surprised to see a good friend.

"Tell me it isn't Kyra Reed of Bare Sophistication Lingerie Boutique," Kiara said with a smile. The two women hugged before Kiara introduced Kyra to Miranda.

"Kyra, this is my friend and old college roommate,

Miranda. Miranda, this is Kyra. We were on a couple of the same panels together at the women empowerment conference I was telling you about a few months ago." Both women greeted each other.

"I've been dying to check out that boutique," Miranda said. "And I know a couple women who took photos at your boudoir studio and they loved how the pictures turned out."

"Thanks," Kyra said with a smile. "We're really excited about how well LA has received the boutique. We're headquartered out of Chicago with a store in Miami as well, so we're hoping to open more locations soon."

"I'm looking at expanding my locations, too," Kiara said. "And I'd love for us to get together and share business ideas, but first, Miranda was just going to explain to me what type of party this was since she knows that I've sworn off men right now. Yet I could have sworn that she mentioned something about renting men."

Kyra's mouth formed a perfect O as she looked from Kiara to Miranda.

Miranda giggled. "About that. I may or may not have left out the part about this party being the first Rent-a-Bachelor silent auction in which a woman can rent a Prescott George bachelor of her choice for up to a week or just a few days."

Kiara's jaw dropped. "You can't be serious! Rent-a-Bachelor? This can't be a real thing."

"Oh, it is," Kyra said. "Girlfriend, why do you think I'm here? My friend and her husband were invited by one of the Moguls, but of course, I'm the single friend, so they brought me along to support the cause. I have no problem with finding a date, but who can pass up the opportunity to rent a sexy piece of chocolate."

Kiara shook her head as she and Miranda laughed at Kyra's candor. She'd only hung out with Kyra a few times, but the girl was nothing if not honest.

Kiara glanced around, noticing for the first time just how many good-looking men filled the room. "I must admit," she said, "there's definitely some good eye candy here."

Kyra nodded. "There truly is. Women are renting bachelors left and right." Kiara and Miranda followed Kyra's outstretched hand that pointed to a corner of the penthouse, where a herd of women stood in front of a row of Apple computers.

"I don't see any men wearing name tags or anything, so I wonder how the women are renting the bachelors," Kiara said.

"Right by the computers, they have an impressive black double-stitched booklet that contains a photo and bio of all single, divorced or widowed eligible Moguls who have agreed to participate," Kyra said. She snagged a glass of wine off the tray of a waiter who passed by, before continuing.

"If you register, you can also see all their info online. Their bio includes their occupation and age, as well as other hobbies that women may want to know. Tonight is the event kickoff, so they have bid assistants to help if you don't want to do the online registration. But going forward, online registration will be the most prominent way to rent bachelors. Since it's a silent auction—and in true Millionaire Mogul fashion—once you make it to the front of the table, one of the bid assistants takes your written bid and contact info. I assume the bachelors predetermine how much time they can give, because some of them are only allowed to be rented for up to two weeks out of a month, while others claim to have the entire month open. Some of the bachelors are so sought-after that they have an open and close bidding time to ensure they aren't double-booked. After you place your bid to rent your guy, for an extra fee, you can receive a small gold pamphlet on the bachelor you rented, as a keepsake. The entire process is really quite nice, because every woman who is willing to lay down some bucks feels like she's won." By the time Kyra was finished talking, Kiara and Miranda were looking at her with blank stares.

"What?" Kyra asked. "I thought you both wanted to know."

Kiara laughed. "How do you know all this? Is it safe to say you rented a bachelor?"

"Girl, please." Kyra reached into her clutch. "I promised one of the bid assistants our newest lingerie set so she could give me the inside scoop. Then I rented two bachelors and brought these sexy gold pamphlets along with them."

"Two dates, huh," Miranda said with a laugh. "Go big, or go home."

Kyra shook her head. "Nope, not dates. I already have my flavor of the month. These hot cakes I just rented will be some great eye candy for a masquerade lingerie event that Bare Sophistication is planning for a women-only eightieth birthday party."

Kyra waved the pamphlets in the air. "Our client was a famous actress back in the 1950s and 1960s and came into our shop a couple months ago saying that she heard about our parties and wanted us to plan one for her. But she didn't just want us to showcase our women's lingerie like we typically do at our masquerade parties. She wanted us to showcase our men's line, equipped with enough eye candy to give her senior citizen friends whiplash. There was no way I was going to turn down this party and my only hope is that I follow in her footsteps when I'm her age. So, I plan to pimp these men out for the one day that I rented them."

Kiara and Miranda were laughing so hard, they didn't hear Vaughn approach. Kiara was grateful that Vaughn introduced himself to Kyra because she still hadn't stopped laughing a few minutes later.

"I must have missed something really funny," Vaughn said, placing a kiss on Miranda's forehead. Kyra just smiled up at him while Kiara and Miranda's laughter finally started to die down. Kiara had been so caught up in Kyra's story, she hadn't noticed the commotion happening near the entrance.

"I wonder what all the fuss is about," Miranda said as they all glanced around the room.

Kiara rose on her tiptoes to try to see over the women in front of her. "Whatever it is, it's clearly the object of some gossip."

"Well, damn," Kyra said as she lightly tapped Kiara on the arm. "I think I see what all the fuss is about."

Kiara glanced toward the direction that Kyra was looking at and froze. Standing toward the front of the penthouse, directly under one of the crystal chandeliers, had to be one of the sexiest men she'd ever seen.

"Oh, wow," she whispered as she soaked in the six-foot-two milk-chocolate-colored man wearing a tailored, deep gray suit with a navy blue BabyBjorn strapped to him and a baby bag hanging off his shoulder.

"You don't see that every day," Miranda said.

"No, you don't." Kiara couldn't take her eyes off him even though he obviously had enough admirers to last a lifetime. His dark hair was closely cropped and his face was clear of any facial hair. Kiara had always been a fan of facial hair, but she had to admit that the clean-shaven look was doing crazy things to her insides.

She couldn't see the baby inside the carrier, but the way he lightly touched the back of the infant's head every so often to make sure the baby was okay caused her ovaries to do a backward flip.

"That's interesting," Miranda said. "For every lustful look he gets from a woman, he's met with a hard and disapproving stare from the men."

"I wonder who that is," Kyra said. "I hope he's a bachelor. But I didn't flip through the bachelor book long enough to spot him."

"There's a reason some of the men aren't very happy with him," Vaughn said. "That's Trey Moore, oldest son of Reginald Moore."

Kiara stole her eyes away to look at Vaughn and Miranda. "The son of the man who caused the LA chapter to be placed on the six-month suspension?"

"In the flesh," Vaughn said. "But I've been working with Trey for some charity events lately, and he's a good guy. He and his two brothers were cleared of any wrongdoings, but I guess some of the members think the apple doesn't fall far from the tree."

"Well, I don't know the story," Kyra said. "But Mr. Daddy Daycare seems to be in the running for tonight's greatest catch. Women are fawning all over him and that baby."

"I don't think he has any kids," Vaughn said. "So, I'm not sure who the baby is. Trey is also the brain behind Rent-a-Bachelor. He's involved with a lot of community outreach for the chapter."

Kiara glanced back at Trey just as his eyes lifted from the baby and locked onto hers. She gasped, caught off guard by the intensity in his gaze. Even from across the room, she could feel the heat.

"Well, well, well." Kyra nudged her. "Looks like our little Kiara has caught someone's eye."

Kiara swallowed, willing her eyes to break contact. *Come on, girl. Why are you still staring at him?* She vaguely heard her friends continuing to chatter around her, but she wasn't comprehending anything they were saying. His gaze had her hypnotized and she was pretty sure she'd never stared at a stranger this long or this deeply before.

"I'm not interested," she said as she finally looked away. She ignored the shared look between Kyra and Miranda. When no one began speaking, she realized they were waiting to call her out on her blatant lie.

"I'm seriously not," she said again, before turning

to Vaughn. "I know this isn't your chapter, but do you think you could give us a quick tour?"

Vaughn nodded. "Sure. The LA members have opened some of the rooms for tours and such tonight anyway. We'll start on the second level."

"Great," Kiara said a little too enthusiastically. When she'd finally agreed to a night out, she'd assumed she would catch up with her friends before their trip to Dubai and maybe have some good old-fashioned adult conversation since the majority of her day was spent around children and babies. What she hadn't signed up for was the most intense eye contact she'd ever had. His eyes had seemed to penetrate right through her, and all she'd wanted to do was tell him to keep on peeling back the layers.

If he could do all that from across the room without even saying two words to her, she didn't want to know what would happen if they actually spoke.

"Who are you looking for?"

Trey turned to face his brother Max. "No one. Just checking out the crowd and seeing who arrived."

Even though they were members of the same chapter and were heavily involved in Prescott George, they weren't particularly close. Their brother Derek was a member as well, but only because their father insisted on paying his membership dues. Trey had always wondered if Reginald paid Derek's dues because he genuinely thought Derek would be a great member, or just for bragging rights to say that all three of his sons were a part of Prescott George.

"The turnout is great," Max said. "Great idea, Trey."

"Thanks. I appreciate it." When Trey had initially presented the idea of having Rent-a-Bachelor as a fund-raising effort to support their big Christmas bash for the chapter, he hadn't expected so many members to be on board given the crazy few months they'd had. Surprisingly, the vote had been unanimous.

Max smiled as he glanced down at Matthew. "And who is this little guy?"

"This is Matthew, Carmen's son, and the reason I had to put you guys on hold a couple days ago when Reginald called." Trey looked from his nephew to Max. "Actually, I was hoping I would see you tonight. I'm sorry to hear about Reginald. How are you holding up?"

Max's smile dropped. "I'm okay given the circumstances. I know that you and Derek don't care for him, but I can't imagine him not being here."

Trey clasped Max's shoulder. "I may not like the man, but I would never wish death on anyone. After I got over the initial shock, I immediately thought about you and how hard I know this will be for you. It's unfortunate, and if you need someone to talk to, I'm here." As the words left his mouth, Trey realized he truly did mean every word. He wanted to be there for Max.

"Thanks, man." Max grew quiet for a few moments before speaking. "I've been meaning to ask you. After the call, some things were sort of left unsaid. I know you and Derek don't owe Reginald anything, but I want to do this for him. I want to investigate this a little more and see if he's innocent like he claims to be, but I don't think I can do it alone. I know we all have demanding schedules, but I can't help but feel like this is something we should all be doing together."

Trey had figured that Max would want to investigate the case for Reginald. He'd had a couple of days to think about the phone call, and although Trey didn't think for one minute that Reginald deserved their help, he couldn't deny the fact that it would weigh heavily on his heart if Reginald was telling the truth and died without them uncovering the real culprit.

"Although I'm not sure I believe that Reginald is innocent, I'd be willing to help investigate further," Trey said. "Maybe we should talk to Derek and meet sometime this week."

"I appreciate this," Max said. "And I already spoke to Derek. I called him this morning. He told me he was sorry that Reginald was dying, but Reginald has never been a part of his life, so he won't help. I know that although he is a member, he isn't actively involved with anything for Prescott George, but I'm hoping that he attends tonight so we can talk."

Trey nodded. "I understand where he's coming from. I may not have the best relationship with Reginald, but Derek went through worse. I think Derek would be willing to meet with us, though. My schedule is swamped, but maybe you could swing by my place this Sunday morning. Are you free?"

Max pulled out his cell phone. "I think so. I can come by before an event I have to appear at. What about Derek?"

"He texted me that he's supposed to be here tonight."

Max's eyes widened. "Really? Derek never attends anything related to Prescott George."

"I was surprised, too," Trey said. "But in case he doesn't show or doesn't stay for long, maybe we should just contact him after the event and see if he's willing to meet with us?"

"Sounds like a plan," Max said.

After they parted ways, Trey was still a little surprised that after all this time, he was finally going to spend some time with his half brothers. Max had once tried to get close to him and Derek, but they both had shut him down. Being the oldest, Trey knew what he had to do. Even if they discovered Reginald was lying about his innocence, it was time for the Moore brothers to finally try to forge a relationship of their own.

Chapter 4

"Come on, beautiful," Trey said to himself. "Where did you go?" He'd been working the room for the past thirty minutes and had already scanned some of the penthouse in search of the brown bombshell in the white dress he'd seen when he'd arrived.

He was about to head to the second level, when he heard someone call out his name. Trey turned around to greet his friend and his wife.

"Kendrick, Nicole. I'm glad you both made it."

"Thanks for inviting us," Kendrick said as the two dabbed fists. "It's a great turnout."

"Thanks, man. How long have you been here?"

"A little over an hour. We brought a friend with us, but we lost her pretty early on."

Trey leaned in to give Nicole a hug, careful not to

crush the baby against his chest. "Hey, Nicole. Beautiful as always."

"Thank you. You look handsome yourself, but I must say that this little guy is stealing all the attention. I haven't seen Matthew since he was two months old. How's Carmen doing?"

"She's good," Trey said. "She got a gig on some new television show, so I'm watching Matthew for her."

"I heard about that," Kendrick said. "Congrats to her."

Trey knew Kendrick from the Hollywood scene and had even written screenplays for a couple of movies that Kendrick had been the creative director of. Now Kendrick and his wife, Nicole, owned an up-and-coming production company.

When all the drama was going on with Reginald, Trey had been able to count on Kendrick and his wife for their support, which was more than he could say for some friends that he'd known his entire life. Kendrick wasn't a member of Prescott George, but he understood all too well how scandals could affect your career, having dealt with his own scandal a while back.

"Are you good, man?" Kendrick asked. Trey didn't have to wonder why he'd asked. This was the first event they'd had for the LA chapter since the suspension was lifted.

"I'm good," Trey said. "Except for the fact that Matthew is getting a little fussy and I've been trying to track down this beautiful woman I saw when I arrived."

"A woman, huh?" Nicole wiggled her eyebrows.

"Was she wearing a beautiful white dress and some gorgeous red pumps?"

Trey squinted his eyes. "How did you guess that?"

Nicole tilted her head to the side. "Because Kendrick and I brought my girl Kyra with us to this event, and right now, Kyra is wearing her Million-Dollar-Matchmaker smile and dragging a woman in a white dress this way."

Trey glanced over his shoulder, his eyes landing on the tall, curvy woman he'd been searching for. Nicole wasn't lying. The other woman did appear to be dragging her his way, but he didn't care as long as he got a closer look.

The white dress she wore fitted her hips and thighs perfectly, but it was her red heels with a strap that wrapped around the ankle that was doing wild things to his imagination. Top that with her silver raindrop necklace that dipped in between her cleavage, and he was sure he'd forget everyone at the party and leave with her if she asked him to.

Her shoulder-length dark brown hair fell in waves around her shoulders, and now that he could see her more closely, he noticed that her cat-shaped eyes seemed to be taking him in just as much as he was.

When they reached them, his throat tightened when he noticed just how plush her red-colored lips were. He could stand there and look at her lips all day. Had Kendrick not nudged him, he probably would have.

"Sorry—what happened?" he asked.

Kendrick shook his head. "Trey, this is our friend Kyra."

"Nice to meet you," Trey said, forcing himself to

focus on the introduction. Kyra was definitely an attractive woman, but Trey couldn't take his eyes off her friend.

"Nice to meet you, too, lover boy," Kyra said with a laugh. "But I'm sure you want to meet my friend Kiara. So—" Kyra lifted Kiara's hand in the air "—Trey, meet Kiara."

Trey wasted no time lifting his hand and enclosing hers in his. When he did, Kiara's eyes shot down to their hands before meeting his gaze again. *That's interesting*, Trey thought. He'd heard about people meeting and feeling sparks when their hands touched, but he'd always thought it was a myth. Looking down at his hand and Kiara's hand, he knew now what those folks had meant. When Kiara removed her hand, he had to refrain from lifting it again.

"It's nice to meet you, Kiara," Trey said.

Kiara smiled. "It's nice to meet you, too, Trey." *Even her voice is sexy.* Kiara's voice was sultry, yet subtle. A combination he'd never really heard before. Had they not been surrounded by their friends, Trey would have bit down on his fist to contain his excitement from hearing his name leave her lips. Instead, he returned her smile, oblivious to the fact that their friends had excused themselves, leaving him alone with Kiara.

"Where did they go?" he asked, looking behind him.

"Kyra pulled them away a few seconds ago as she muttered some inappropriate things," Kiara said. "Therefore, I won't dare repeat them."

Trey laughed, remembering how Kyra had introduced them. "I'm guessing subtlety isn't her strong suit."

Kiara shook her head. "Not at all. I doubt *subtlety* is even in her vocabulary."

"We all need at least one friend like that," Trey said. "And I'm glad she introduced us. I've been trying to find you all night."

"I doubt that," she said.

"I was. Ever since I walked in and spotted you from across the room."

Kiara glanced away. "I'm not interested."

Okay, maybe that last line was a little cheesy. But it's true. "You're not?"

"No," she said, meeting him with a cold stare. "It may have seemed like I was staring, but it was only because I was trying to figure out who you were."

Trey studied her eyes for any sign that she wasn't being honest. Ever since Reginald had been expelled from Prescott George, he'd run into a few women who knew the story and treated him as if he were his father. It only took one look into Kiara's eyes to realize she'd heard the story and was also passing judgment.

But she genuinely looked interested earlier tonight, he thought. *No way I imagined the look she had in her eye.* Trey could admit that he'd once misjudged a woman's interest in him, but that was way back in college and it had only happened that one time. Tonight, he'd felt the way Kiara had been staring at him all the way to his bones.

"He's adorable," Kiara said as she looked down at Matthew. "And he's getting fussy."

Trey bounced a little in place to try to calm down Matthew. "Yeah, I think it's past his bedtime, but I can't get him to fall asleep. He's my nephew and I'm babysitting him for a couple weeks, but I have no idea what I'm doing."

On cue, Matthew started wailing, gaining attention from people standing near them. Trey tried to remain calm, but he couldn't figure out how to console him. Finally getting an idea, Trey reached in his pocket to pull out a pacifier, but Kiara swooped in, pulled Matthew out of the carrier and was already calming him down.

"Do you have a blanket or anything for me to cover my dress?" she asked.

Trey fumbled with the baby bag and pulled out a blanket. "Here you go." He draped the blanket over her shoulder. "It took me over an hour to put that carrier together, and you unsnap him from it like it's a piece of cake. You're really great with babies."

"I should be," Kiara said with a laugh. "I own LA Little Ones Daycare and Preschool, so I'm around babies all day."

"I've heard of LA Little Ones," Trey said. "Quite a few folks in the film industry take their kids to your day care."

Kiara looked up from Matthew. "You work in television?"

"I'm a screenwriter," Trey said, as a thought came to mind. "And you may be the answer to my prayers. I only have a couple weeks to finish my screenplay, and it's hard to do that with an infant. Placing him in a day care for the daytime would help me tremendously."

"I would love to help you out, but I can't. The current wait for an open slot in my day care is twelve months."

"You're kidding me," Trey said. "A twelve-month

wait? Any chance you can make an exception? I know we just met, but you'd be doing me a huge favor."

Kiara was shaking her head before Trey finished his plea. "Sorry—wish I could. But if I make an exception for you, I'd have to make an exception for others." Once Matthew was completely calm, Kiara placed him back in the carrier.

"I understand," Trey said, deflated. "I apologize for asking for special treatment. That usually isn't like me. It's just been a stressful few months, so I'm not completely myself."

Kiara's eyes softened. "I know it's not my place to ask, but is your stress because of what your father did?"

Trey frowned. He'd suspected her hot-and-cold behavior toward him was because she'd heard about the suspension and knew Reginald was his father, but it didn't make having her ask any easier. "Unfortunately, yes, Reginald is my father, but we aren't that close."

Trey blinked, surprised that he'd shared that fact. He usually kept any thoughts about Reginald to himself.

"It must be even harder since you aren't that close," Kiara said. "I assume that if you were, you'd expect for people to associate you with your father. But since you aren't, you're guilty by association with a man you don't have a close relationship with."

Trey nodded. "I've never heard someone put it so clearly. Yes, that's exactly it. And honestly, I don't care for the man. To be investigated and have my character questioned was embarrassing and infuriating. To top it off, Reginald called all his sons to claim his innocence and asked us for our help to prove it. Why he feels privileged enough to even contact us is beyond my understanding. But of course, I will probably agree to help because what type of son would I be if I refuse to help him and prove that I'm no better than he is?"

The words were out of his mouth before he had a chance to reel them back in. Trey's frustrated eyes caught Kiara's understanding ones. *Why the hell did I just tell her all that?* He really needed to take a vacation after he turned in his screenplay because he had no doubt he was slowly losing his mind and, apparently, losing his filter, too.

"I'm sorry," he said. "I'm usually a more private person, but like I said, it's been a stressful few months."

Kiara reached out her hand to touch Trey's. "It's okay. I'm glad you told me." Her fingers began moving in small circles over his skin, the heat from her touch making him wish he could keep her hands right where they were, all night.

"Tell you what," she said. "This one time, I'll make an exception and accept Matthew into LA Little Ones for the next two weeks."

"Thank you," Trey said with a grateful smile. "You have no idea how much I appreciate this."

Kiara laughed. "Don't thank me yet. You don't know how much it costs. LA Little Ones isn't cheap."

"I had a feeling it wasn't." Trey leaned closer to Kiara, immediately soaking in the sweet scent of her perfume. "I'm willing to pay whatever it costs because I'm grateful for your help."

"You're welcome, but I'm not only doing this for you." Kiara looked at Matthew, who was now sleeping soundly.

"I'm doing this for Matthew's sake." She tugged at the contraption holding up the infant. "The BabyBjorn is inside out and a couple clips are configured wrong. At this rate, there's no way you can babysit by yourself."

Her eyes were teasing, but Trey also knew there was some truth to what she was saying. He hoped that she realized he didn't care if Matthew was the real reason she'd agreed to help him out, because accepting Matthew into her day care meant that she would be seeing a lot more of him whether she wanted to or not.

Chapter 5

"Here we are, M-dog," Trey said as he pulled into the parking lot of LA Little Ones. Trey wasn't sure what he suspected, but the upscale day care was a lot larger than he'd thought it would be.

When Trey walked through the doors of the place, he smiled as he was immediately greeted by the sweet smell of baby lotion. The lobby was painted in soft pastels, and although he couldn't really see past the front desk, he could tell the colors and design were constant throughout.

"Welcome to LA Little Ones," the receptionist said. "Do you have an appointment?"

"Yes," he said. "My name is Trey Moore. Kiara Woods is expecting me at this time."

The receptionist typed a few keys. "I see your appointment, sir. If you wait here, I'll call Ms. Woods for you."

Trey only had to wait a couple of minutes before Kiara arrived. "Hello, Mr. Moore. You can follow me to my office."

"Of course," he said, trying to maintain his composure. Trey wasn't sure what it was about this woman, but Kiara's beauty kicked him in the gut in a way a woman never had before.

Today, she was wearing a flowy peach dress and brown sandals, giving him the first peek of her French-tip-painted toenails. Matthew made a gurgling noise, reminding him that he was here for his nephew and not to soak in Kiara's beauty.

"On our way to my office, I'll give you a quick tour," Kiara said as she glanced over her shoulder. The move instantly made Trey envision her spread on all fours, glancing over her shoulder in the same way. *Okay, so maybe I'm here to soak in her beauty as well.*

"Here's the main room for our newborns and infants." Kiara pointed to a room with crisp white cribs all lined in two rows and a cream-colored wall. In one corner were several rocking chairs, and in the other, a plush rug and huge stuffed animals. "Through those double doors are two additional rooms for infants and it's equipped with its own large bathroom."

Trey peeked into the room, noticing that almost all the cribs were full.

"And this is our main toddler room and activity center," Kiara said as she walked down the hall. "This space also has two additional rooms and its own private bathroom. Infants and toddlers react best to any semblance of familiarity, so the warm colors and the type of cognitive and visual activities we provide at LA Little Ones will follow the child throughout their time in our program."

As they walked through the day care and preschool, Kiara explained their nutritional program and showed him the preschool area in the second wing of the building. As she'd stated, he noticed consistency throughout the tour.

"Trey, I'd like for you to meet Monica," Kiara said when they made their way back to the infant room. "Monica is the nursery director and my eyes and ears when I'm not here."

Trey extended a hand. "Nice to meet you, Monica."

"You as well," she said, accepting his handshake.

Kiara waved over another woman. "Trey, I'd like for you to meet Penny. She'll be the nurse assigned to Matthew during his time with us. We will be sending you live updates on Matthew throughout the day. At the end of the week, you'll receive a detailed report on Matthew's diet, health, sleeping patterns during naps and any additional findings we see fit to share."

Trey greeted Penny as well, impressed by the professionalism of the staff and the entire operation.

"You can leave Matthew with Penny," Kiara said. "And then we'll head back to my office and discuss additional details."

Trey did as Kiara suggested. Once they were in Kiara's office, Trey finally let out an appreciative whistle.

"Wow. This is more like a luxury hotel for kids than

a day-care center and preschool. I am thoroughly impressed and I can see why the wait to be a part of LA Little Ones is twelve months long."

"Thank you." Kiara smiled and motioned for Trey to take a seat, while she sat behind her desk. "I'll admit that I was hoping the day care would be in high demand when I started the business, but I had no idea to what lengths some people would go to get their child placed here."

"What do you mean?"

Kiara pointed to a locked file cabinet in the corner of her office. "That cabinet is filled with couples who are currently trying to conceive or have plans to try soon and want to leave deposits one to three years out for their future child to be accepted into our program."

"Get out of here," Trey said. "Although that's surprising, you should be extremely proud of everything you've accomplished."

Kiara glanced around her office. "I am, but it's not just me. I have an amazing staff who believed in my vision and saw the potential before anyone else did. A lot of my staff have been with me since the beginning. Without them, I'm not sure I would have reached this level of success so soon."

Trey observed Kiara as she went into more detail about how certain staff members contributed to the vision. She'd been such a maddening mix of friendly and aloof last night at the auction, he hadn't been sure if he'd imagined her initial interest, or if she was just trying to appear to be indifferent.

"Have dinner with me at my place tonight," he said, cutting her off.

Kiara's eyes widened. "What? You want me to come by your place? But we just met last night."

Okay, she has a point there. Trey wasn't really the type to invite a woman whom he'd only just met to his house, but he wanted to get to know Kiara more. "I wouldn't originally suggest my place so soon, but I have to babysit Matthew, so I can't leave my home tonight. Plus, I could use your baby whisperer insight."

"Oh," she said, perking up in her chair. "So, you want me to come over to act as some sort of nanny informant for Matthew?"

"No, not at all. I just wanted to get to know you and figured learning more about how to care for my nephew would be a bonus." Trey's eyes briefly dropped to her lips. He had every intention of taking a quick peek, but noticed, for the first time since he'd arrived, that she was wearing light pink lipstick. By the time his eyes had ventured back to hers, he was sure she could feel the heat reflected in his gaze.

Just like last night, he couldn't look away from her no matter how hard he tried. Kiara broke eye contact first. "I told you last night that I wasn't interested."

Trey chuckled. "I remember what you said. But there's no harm in us getting to know one another better as *friends*, is there?" The last thing he wanted was to be Kiara's friend. He had enough of those. However, he was willing to keep things PG if it meant she'd stop by his place tonight.

"You won't try any funny business?" Kiara asked, crossing her arms over her chest.

"Nope." Trey lifted his hand. "Scout's honor."

Kiara leaned a little closer, studying his eyes. He let her look her fill and tried his best to mask the real reason he wanted her to stop by his place. He'd known her less than twenty-four hours, and already, he feared he was slightly addicted to her company.

"Okay," she said. "I'll stop by tonight for dinner."

A grin crept onto Trey's lips. "Perfect. I look forward to it."

Girl, what are you doing? Don't get out of your car! Kiara's thoughts had been racksacking her brain for the past twenty minutes, reminding her that having dinner with Trey Moore was a *very* bad idea.

Even worse, she was randomly moving her lips to appear to be talking on the phone just in case Trey glanced outside his window and spotted her.

"It's official," she said to herself. "You've officially gone off the deep end." It was one thing to avoid relationships based off the heartbreak she'd already experienced. However, she'd hit a new low by pretending to be on the phone to avoid going into a man's home for dinner.

He's not just any man, she thought. *He's a sexy man who spends more time looking deeply into your eyes than he actually spends talking to you.* Kiara had never dated a man like Trey before. Granted, she didn't really know what type of man he was, but she had a feeling that he was the type a girl could get addicted to. The type who noticed little things about you that others failed to see.

Dating Trey would consume me. Kiara sat upright in her seat as the thought crossed her mind. "Date him?" He'd invited her to one dinner, and already, she was thinking about dating him.

"This is crazy," she said, getting out of her car. "You're a smart and successful woman, so surely you can handle dinner with a man and not think it means you're headed down the relationship road."

Kiara rang the doorbell, mentally giving herself one more pep talk before Trey answered the door in black sweats and a white T-shirt. He had a screaming infant cradled in his arms.

"Come on in," Trey said, stepping aside from the door. "M-dog was fine, and then ten minutes ago, he just started crying and hasn't stopped since."

Kiara briefly looked Trey up and down. Even in the chaos with his nephew, the man looked delicious. "When was the last time his diaper was changed?"

Trey's eyes widened. "I can't remember. I was writing and cooking dinner while he took a nap. So, I guess a few hours ago."

Kiara peeked into his diaper. "He needs to be changed. That's all." Kiara made quick work of changing the diaper, and as soon as she was finished, happy Matthew was back.

"You're amazing," Trey said. "I can't believe I didn't think of something as simple as a diaper change."

"It happens," she said with a laugh.

"I would love for you to teach me some more skills.

Being responsible for another life is not easy. I mean, M-dog seems fine, but I have no idea what I'm doing."

"Yes, it can be daunting at times," Kiara said. "But you'll get the hang of it and Matthew seems to be doing okay. What's with the M-dog reference?"

"That's my nickname for him. My sister hates it, but I think it's pretty cool."

Kiara rolled her eyes. "Of course you do. It's the type of nickname a man would give a baby. God forbid you call him Matt or Matty."

Trey frowned. "She calls him Matty and I think it's terrible. He'll hate that nickname by the time he reaches high school."

Kiara shrugged. "I guess you're right." She sniffed the air and smelled a hint of something burning. "Is that our dinner?"

"Oh, crap." Trey handed Matthew back to Kiara and rushed to the kitchen. Matthew grabbed ahold of Kiara's pointer finger when she lightly tapped his nose.

"I think your uncle burned dinner," she said in a baby voice.

"You'd be correct," Trey said, walking back into the living room. "Any chance you'd be down for takeout?"

"Sounds good to me," she said with a laugh. Any nervousness Kiara had been feeling left the moment she'd opened the door and seen Trey in a panic.

An hour later, they'd finished their takeout and Matthew was sound asleep in his crib.

"He really is precious," Kiara said, a familiar ache in her heart. "Your sister is a lucky woman."

Trey looked down at Matthew. "Yeah, he's pretty

amazing." Trey looked back to her. "You look stunning tonight."

Kiara swallowed. "You saw me in this outfit earlier today."

"And you looked stunning in it earlier as well. I was so impressed by LA Little Ones that I forgot to mention how impressed I was with you as well."

Oh, Lord. If Trey kept up these compliments, she would never be able to slow the rapid beating of her heart.

"Thank you. You looked handsome in your suit earlier today and you look nice now, too." Kiara's eyes glanced over him again. *Girl, that's the biggest lie you've told in a while*, she thought. *You know he looks better than nice. The man exudes great sex and everything fantasies are made of.*

"Now that we have some time," Trey said, "would you like a tour of my home?"

"I'd love one."

"Great." Trey stood and grabbed the second baby monitor off the table before he reached out his hand to help Kiara up. "We'll start with my favorite room in the house."

Kiara followed Trey up a set of spiral stairs that were separate from the stairs that led to the second level. When they reached the top, Trey led Kiara through a narrow hallway to a grand loft space that took her breath away.

"Oh my gosh," she said, taking in the lush greenery and skylight windows that she was sure offered a lot of sunlight in the daytime. "I can't believe you own a greenhouse. This is beautiful."

"Thank you," Trey said as he walked down a path leading to a set of large doors. "I made sure my architect included this space in my blueprints as soon as I purchased the lot for this house. I call it my serenity space because it's where I come to clear my mind."

Kiara eagerly peeked over Trey's shoulder when he opened the doors to reveal a breathtaking rooftop terrace.

"I didn't get a chance to clean and dust this area today. Otherwise, I would have insisted that we eat up here."

"Wow," Kiara said, momentarily speechless. The greenery from inside continued outdoors, except there was also a very nice wooden table, sofa and chairs, an outdoor fireplace structure, and if she wasn't mistaken, a Jacuzzi in a secluded corner of the terrace.

"I can see why this is your favorite place," Kiara said. "I can't imagine ever leaving this area if this were my home."

"Trust me, it's hard to leave sometimes." Trey motioned for her to join him on the mahogany wicker sofa with plush white cushions. He placed the baby monitor on the outdoor table before he opened a glass cooler located near the sofa.

"Would you like a glass of red wine?"

"Sure," she said.

Trey pulled out some chilled wine and two wineglasses, briefly glancing at her as he poured. "I'm glad you like the terrace," he said, handing her a glass. "I don't take many people up here."

Kiara took a sip, welcoming the cool liquid. It was a little nippy out, but she couldn't even feel the chill with all the heat they were generating. "I feel honored that you showed me your place of serenity. Thank you."

"You're welcome." Trey watched her over the edge of his glass as he took a sip of his wine as well. *There he goes again*, she thought. *Staring at me with those almost-black eyes.* Kiara didn't think she'd ever met someone with eyes as dark and deep as Trey's. When he looked at her the way he did now, she had to make a conscious effort to try to calm the swarm of bees buzzing around in her stomach.

"Tell me more about yourself," she said. "Have you always wanted to be a screenplay writer?"

"For as long as I can remember," he said proudly. "I guess you can say I grew up in the business. My mother, Vivian Lashay, is an actress, so I've been a part of Hollywood since I was young."

Kiara smiled. "I've seen your mom in a few television shows and movies. She's really talented."

"Thank you. My sister, Carmen, and I certainly think so."

Kiara thought back to the conversation she'd had with him at the Rent-a-Bachelor event. "When we met, you mentioned that your father called his sons to ask for help. Do you and your sister have different fathers?"

"Yes, we do. I'm Reginald's oldest son, but he had two more from two different women, so I have two half brothers. After he and my mom split, she met my stepdad, Frank, and had my sister. My stepdad is cool, but I never really felt like I had a father. Reginald was an absentee father, and although I appreciate my stepdad for being around, he had his hands full with my sister and Mom."

"That's unfortunate, but I understand," Kiara said. "When I was a young girl, I thought the sun rose and set over my father. I'm the oldest of four, but after my youngest brother was born, he split without a word. That was the last we heard from him. My mom raised us on her own, but since she had two jobs, I spent a lot of my childhood raising my two brothers and sister."

"That must have been hard," Trey said, taking another sip of wine. "For me, I never had a relationship with Reginald. But in your case, you were close to your father, at least until he left."

Kiara shrugged. "Yeah, it was hard. However, as you proved, a lot of people have struggled with absentee parents. Unfortunately, I didn't seem to learn anything from that experience because I ended up marrying someone who I now know shared a lot of similarities with my father. Had I noticed that before he proposed, maybe I could have saved myself the heartache and divorce that followed."

Oh, crap. Why did I say that? Kiara took a big sip of her wine. *Mentioning your divorce on a first date counts as overshare.*

"No, it doesn't," Trey said, confusing her. "I don't mind hearing about your divorce if you want to share. In fact, I want to know the story."

Kiara's jaw slightly dropped. "Please tell me I didn't just voice my thoughts aloud."

"Okay, then," he said with a sly smile. "I won't tell you. But I meant what I said. Whenever you're ready to talk about your divorce, I'm all ears." He held her gaze and lightly picked up her free hand, placing a soft kiss on the back of it. "I know we just met, but I'm thoroughly intrigued by you, Kiara Woods."

Kiara looked from her hand to his before downing the rest of her wine. "I think we should save that story for our next date." She briefly closed her eyes. "I mean meeting. We can save that story for our next meeting." Kiara stood abruptly. "I think it's time for me to go before I spill all my guts on your rooftop terrace."

"Okay," Trey said with a laugh. "I'll walk you out."

They made their way through the greenhouse and down the spiral stairs. Trey checked on Matthew while Kiara gathered her purse and light sweater.

"I had a nice time tonight," Kiara said when she reached the door. When she didn't hear a response, she turned around to find him watching her intently.

"I had a nice time as well." Trey took a step closer to her. "I enjoyed getting to know you a little better." He was so close, Kiara was afraid to breathe.

"Me, too," she whispered. His eyes dropped to her lips and stayed there for a while. After a few moments, she forced herself to swallow the lump in her throat.

He took another step closer, so she took another step back, only to be met with the door. When his hand reached up to cup her face, Kiara completely froze. *There's no way he's going to kiss me, right? We just met each other.*

"Do you want me to stop?" he asked.

Say yes. Say yes. Say yes. "No," she said, moments before his lips came crashing down onto hers. Her hands flew to the back of his neck as he gently pushed her against the door. Kiara had experienced plenty of first kisses in the past, but this was unlike any first kiss she'd ever had. Trey's lips were soft, yet demanding. Eager, yet controlled. When she parted her lips to get a better taste, his tongue briefly swooped into her mouth before he ended their kiss with a soft peck and backed away.

Kiara couldn't be sure how she looked, but she certainly felt unhinged and downright aroused.

"Come on," Trey said with a nod. "I'll walk you to your car."

How is he even functioning after that kiss? Kiara felt like she glided to the car, rather than walked. Yet Trey looked as composed as ever.

"We should get together again soon," he said, opening her car door. Kiara sat down in the driver's seat and looked up at him. He flashed her a sexy smile.

"And for the record, this was definitely a date," Trey said with a wink. "I didn't stop kissing you because I wasn't enjoying it, nor was I trying to tease you. I stopped kissing you because if I hadn't, I'd be ready to drag you into my bedroom. Which also brings me to the reason I didn't show you my bedroom. I didn't trust myself not to make a move." He leaned a little closer. "When we make love, I want us to know one another a little better, so I forced myself to stop kissing you tonight and it was damn hard to do so. Have a good night, Kiara."

Trey softly kissed her cheek and closed her door before she could vocalize a response. Quite frankly, she didn't think she had anything to say anyway. Her mind was still reeling and her lips were still tingling from that explosive kiss.

Kiara gave a quick wave. *I told you not to get out the car earlier*, that voice in her head teased. She started her car and drove away from Trey's house.

"What the hell just happened?" She'd originally thought that she could avoid him or keep their relationship strictly friendly. Now she wasn't so sure. Kissing Trey had awakened desires she thought she'd long buried. Feelings she'd ignored and pushed aside.

Kiara made it to her home a few minutes later. She glanced at her house before dropping her head to the steering wheel. She was in deep and she knew it. To make matters worse, she only lived a five-minute drive from Trey's house, meaning there was no way she was getting any sleep tonight knowing a man that sexy was only a couple of miles away.

Chapter 6

"You like that, huh, M-dog?" Trey danced across his kitchen as baby Matthew sat on the floor in his car seat, laughing up at him.

Trey wasn't sure what he loved about Sunday mornings, but Sunday never failed to put him in a good mood. Considering that his brothers were due to arrive at his place in ten minutes, he needed to keep his energy up. He doubted any of them wanted to talk about Reginald, but Trey was glad that Derek had agreed to meet with him and Max, and deep down, he knew they all realized this conversation was much needed.

Matthew continued to laugh as Trey took out the containers of breakfast he'd picked up from a local diner and placed them on the large island in the kitchen. LA Little Ones was a lifesaver, but he was glad to have

Matthew with him this Sunday. Being with the little dude was making him realize that he may actually want to be a father one day. The jury was still out, but it was originally something he'd never wanted. Now he wasn't so sure. He was getting the hang of this parenting thing…sort of.

Trey's mind drifted to Kiara as it had been since the night he met her. She had so many personality traits that he liked and admired, but her luscious lips were the reason he was having trouble sleeping at night. He hadn't planned on kissing her at the end of the night, but a wave of potent want had come over him so hard that he knew he couldn't let her walk out that door without giving him a taste of her sweetness.

Once he'd committed to the kiss, the only thing that would have stopped him would have been if Kiara didn't want it as much as he did. Had she told him to stop, he would have. Instead, she'd only been even more responsive to his lips on hers, and the sweet moans that were coming from her mouth almost made him forget that he had to maintain some semblance of control.

The doorbell rang, interrupting his thoughts and his dance routine. "Hey, Max," Trey said, greeting his brother. "Come on in."

"Hey, Trey. Derek just pulled up, too."

Trey glanced over Max's shoulder in time to see Derek get out of his car and head to the front door.

"Hey, man," he said, dabbing fists with Derek. "Glad you could make it."

"I didn't want to come," Derek said honestly. "But you're right. The three of us need to talk this out."

Once inside, Trey led both the men into the kitchen, where he'd laid out the food.

"Is this from Lou's Diner right outside Hollywood?" Max asked.

Trey nodded. "Sure is."

"I used to go to this joint all the time," Derek said. "Best breakfast in LA." Trey smiled, not surprised that they all liked the same breakfast spot.

"Is this your nephew?" Derek asked.

Trey looked at Matthew, who'd fallen asleep. "Yes, this is M-dog. I'm watching him for a while for my sister."

A few minutes after the men resumed eating, Trey addressed the elephant in the room. "I think we can all agree that in the past few months it's been pretty stressful to be a Moore."

"That's an understatement," Derek said with a forced laugh.

"True," Max said. "It's been pretty tough. But I believe Reginald when he says he's innocent. He may lie about a lot of things, but I don't think he'd lie about this."

"Right," Derek said sarcastically. "Let's not forget that the man didn't even acknowledge me for most of my childhood. He's such a stand-up guy."

"Sorry," Max said. "That's not what I meant."

Derek shrugged. "It's cool. You always take up for him. I'm used to it."

Trey looked from Derek to Max, hoping the start of this conversation wasn't a reflection on how the rest of it would go.

"Listen, guys," Trey said. "We've spent our entire lives

letting our relationship with Reginald come between our bond as brothers. Derek, I understand why you're upset. Reginald wasn't in our lives, and for that reason, we really don't owe him anything. Max, I'll be the first to admit that I didn't want to build a relationship with you because every time we spoke, you would only want to take up for Reginald and couldn't seem to understand that he didn't treat Derek and me like he treated you."

Trey looked at both men before continuing. "But Reginald is dying, and although I dislike the man, if there is a chance that he's innocent, I don't want him to die without the truth coming out."

"I'm sorry," Max said. "I know you guys didn't have it easy growing up and I didn't know I always came across that way. To be honest, I just wanted to have a relationship with my older brothers. That's all."

Some of the tension in Derek's shoulders released. "I know that," Derek said. "Back then, I was too stubborn and hurt to even think about having a relationship with either of you."

"We've all made some mistakes in the past. And I still can't believe I'm saying this, but now is the time for us to come together." Trey looked at Derek. "We'd be a better team if the three of us work together on this. So, Derek, what do you say? Are you in?"

Matthew's loud wail echoed against the walls before Derek could respond. Trey immediately picked him up out of his car seat and brought him over to where his brothers were sitting just as his cell phone rang.

"Can one of you hold him while I get that?"

"Sure," Derek said with a nod.

Trey was relieved when he glanced at his phone. He'd been waiting on this call. "Hey, Pete. Tell me you have good news."

"I do," Pete said on the other line. "I was able to hack into the San Diego chapter's server and I can already tell others have been here, too. Hackers always leave crumbs behind and the really cocky ones even like to leave their trademark in some way. It will take some digging, but once I have more info, I'll be able to trace the hacker and get you a name."

"That would be great," Trey said. "My brothers and I would be able to handle it from there." Trey got a few more details from Pete before disconnecting the call.

"Was that about Reginald's case?" Max asked.

"It was. I have a friend who's following the trail of the files that were hacked from the San Diego chapter. If he can find the hacker, it's possible we can figure out who hired them."

"Sounds good," Max said. "I'm following up on a few leads, too."

They both looked to Derek, who was engrossed with baby Matthew. "I can feel both your eyes on me," Derek said without raising his head. "I'm assuming you both have already started digging."

"We have," Trey said. "Max called the other day and mentioned that we have to consider the possibility that Reginald was framed by someone in the LA chapter."

"Have you given any more thought to helping us?" Max asked.

Derek sighed, looking from one man to the other. "Let me be honest in saying that the only thing I think this investigation will prove is that Reginald was indeed behind sabotaging the San Diego chapter." He glanced back down at Matthew, who was now interested in playing with Derek's watch. "And I'm not doing this for him. I'm doing this for both of you, and I guess, a little for me, too. Just because Reginald was never a father to me, it doesn't mean I can turn my back on the situation."

Trey and Max shared a hopeful look. "Does that mean you'll help us?" Max asked.

"Yes, I'll help."

Trey walked to stand between Derek and Max and placed a hand on each of their shoulders. Now was the time for him to say something else insightful, but honestly, Trey was content to soak in the moment without any words.

"Is now a good time to let you both know that Reginald would like us to stop over soon?" Max asked, breaking the silence.

Derek shook his head. "Let me guess. You told him about this meeting and he assumed we'd all agree to help with the investigation?"

"Something like that," Max said. "He didn't assume, but he was hopeful."

Trey looked at Derek and the two shared a laugh. There was nothing funny about the situation, but it was nice to laugh about it to break up the tension.

The world worked in mysterious ways, and Trey would be the first to admit that it was strange to feel a closeness to men he'd never really had in his life before, talking about a man whose name he purposely tried to leave out of his mouth.

"Max," Trey said. "How about we exchange notes regarding any efforts we've already begun initiating and fill Derek in on everything?"

"That's a good start," Max said before diving into the details. Halfway through his explanation, he was interrupted by a series of messages pinging on his phone.

"Oh, no," Max said, reading the messages. "Looks like the meeting may happen sooner than we think. Can you both spare an hour right now?"

"Why?" Trey asked. "Is that Reginald?"

"Yeah," Max said, frowning. "He says he woke up pretty sick and was hoping to talk to us today instead."

Trey shook his head. It was just like Reginald to expect them all to work off his time. He was about to tell him that he couldn't meet today since he needed to work on his screenplay, but Derek spoke up, surprising them both.

"Let's go," Derek said. "Let's meet with him today. If we're doing this investigation right, we need to hear all the details from the horse's mouth. It's one thing to claim you're innocent, but his alibis didn't check out and I want to know why. He also needs to understand that we won't be at his beck and call."

Max and Derek looked to Trey. "Okay," Trey said. "You both head to his place and M-dog and I will meet you there."

Derek was right. They needed to get this meeting over with.

Trey glanced down at Matthew, who was in his car seat and still fascinated by his toy keys.

"Reginald, you have to try and understand," Trey

said for the third time in the past hour. "We need you to document anything that you previously told the Prescott George board about the San Diego sabotages. We have the files that state what you said, but the only way to know if some of your words were twisted or changed on the doctored files is if you tell us what happened again in your own words."

"I already told you," Reginald said, his voice slightly carrying. "For some of the nights you're asking me about, I had alibis. For other nights, I can't remember. But I didn't do what they're claiming I did."

Reginald leaned back in his grand desk chair and sighed. "I've reached out to every man who I once considered a friend and who I assumed would know I'm innocent, and with the exception of a couple, they've all turned their backs on me. After all the time I committed to Prescott George, they were willing to throw away our friendship at the first sign of trouble."

When Reginald coughed, Trey cringed. It didn't sound good and Trey could visibly see how much frailer Reginald looked from the last time he'd seen him. Even when they'd arrived at his Malibu mansion, he hadn't appeared to stand as tall as he once did. He hadn't shaken their hands as strongly as he once had. He hadn't even had as much strength and power in his voice as Trey remembered. Trey hadn't realized it had gotten this bad, and one look at Derek and he could tell he felt it, too. They may have never been close to Reginald, but Reginald had always seemed like the type of tall and powerful black man who would live forever.

"I know I'm not helping," Reginald said when his

coughing died down. He stood from his chair and leaned both hands on his grand maple desk. "I'm aware that I'm asking my boys to perform a miracle on my behalf when I've never been that great a father." Reginald looked from Max, to Derek, to Trey. "The truth is, I don't deserve sons as good as you and one of my biggest regrets is that I was never a true father to Derek and Trey. My lack of responsibility and duty as a father pushed my sons farther apart when all of you should have had the opportunity to be in one another's lives."

"That part wasn't just on you," Trey said. "We could have worked harder at having a better relationship with one another, but we didn't."

Reginald opened his mouth to speak, but instead, he went into another coughing fit. Max went to his side to help him sit back down in his chair. Watching Max and Reginald together made Trey's heart ache for a different reason than it used to.

Despite the circumstances, Trey couldn't imagine losing a mother to cancer like Max had a few years ago, just to turn around and have a father diagnosed with a different form of cancer.

"How about we let you get some rest," Derek suggested. "The three of us can get together and work through some of the things you discussed with us today."

"I agree with that," Max said. "You need your rest, Dad."

Reginald took a sip of water. "Okay, that works. There was just one other thing I wanted to discuss with each of you while I have you all together." All three brothers remained silent as they waited for Reginald to continue.

"You don't have to give me an answer now," Reginald said. "But I would really love to have each of you over for Thanksgiving dinner here at my home. I know it's asking a lot of you, but all I ask is that you think about it."

Trey's face remained neutral, although internally, he was shocked that Reginald had asked them all to spend a holiday with him. Back when Trey was a kid, he would have given anything to have an invite to celebrate a holiday with his biological father.

They all agreed to think about it, and ten minutes later, Trey and Matthew were headed home. "Well, M-dog," Trey said aloud. "We survived our first meeting with the brothers and Reginald. How about I spend the rest of our Sunday working on my screenplay and you spend the rest of it sleeping? Deal?" In response, Matthew blew spit bubbles.

Trey laughed. "Should I take that as a yes or no?" An incoming call redirected Trey's attention.

"Hello, this is Trey Moore."

"Hi, Mr. Moore. This is Lacey, one of the bid assistants for Rent-a-Bachelor."

Trey clenched his wheel a little harder. *Crap, how could I forget about this?* Although he was proud the Rent-a-Bachelor program was a success, he'd forgotten that he'd opened one day this week for him to be rented. The timing was horrible, but he felt as though he had to give up at least one day to the initiative since he was the brain behind the operation. "Yes, Lacey. What can I do for you?"

"I was calling to let you know that you've been rented for Monday night. Are you still available tomorrow?"

Trey refrained from grinding his teeth. *No, I'm not free. I have the next blockbuster sitting on my desk and I must get to it.* "Yes, I'm still free," he said.

"Great," Lacey said. "You've been rented by a Ms. Kiara Woods."

Trey cleared his throat. "Did you say *Kiara Woods*?"

"Yes, sir. I will send you the additional details to your email."

"Thank you, Lacey. Have a good day."

"You, too, sir."

Trey disconnected the call and glanced at Matthew through the mirror. "Did you hear that, M-dog? Looks like Uncle Trey has a date with Kiara tomorrow. So, you know what that means, right?" Matthew waved his toy keys in the air.

"How about I just tell you," Trey said. "That means I need you to be a good boy tomorrow and go to bed a little early. Can you do that for me?" Matthew threw his keys on the floor.

"Nope, wrong answer, M-dog."

Chapter 7

Unlike the last time she'd arrived at Trey's, she had no problem getting out of the car. All Kiara had needed was a little time to put everything in perspective. Now that she had, she felt much more confident in her ability to keep things with Trey friendly.

Just don't forget why you're here tonight, she reminded herself as she gathered a couple of bags from her car. She was woman enough to admit that the kiss they'd shared had rocked her world. However, there were still so many more things that Trey didn't know about her. Things that she knew would be deal breakers as they had for relationships in her past.

She approached the front door and rang the doorbell. Trey answered shortly after, wearing dark jeans and a navy V-neck shirt. She could smell his freshly showered scent from where she stood on the doorstep. When her eyes made their way to his face, she was surprised to see him wearing stylish black-rimmed glasses.

"Come on in." He stepped aside so she could enter. "I was surprised to hear that you rented me for the night and wanted to meet at my place instead of yours. Dinner is almost ready."

Dinner? She glanced around the living room and kitchen and noticed dinner warming on the stove, two wineglasses sitting on the counter next to a bottle of wine, and Matthew playing in his crib.

"You made dinner?" she asked.

"Of course. I had to make up for the other night. I was hoping we could eat outside on the terrace, but I don't want to take Matthew out there with us and it's a little chilly. So maybe we can start dinner here and make our way to the roof later."

"Oh, no," Kiara said, placing the bags on the floor next to his sofa. "No rooftop tonight. I came here to handle some business." She leaned down to reach into one of the bags.

Trey scrunched his forehead. "What's all this?"

"This is the answer to your prayers," she said. Kiara handed him a thick green binder. "I call this my baby bible, and it contains everything you need to know about how to care for a child, starting with newborns. Tonight, I figured I could show you how to properly care for Matthew since you're a fish out of water at times."

Trey blinked. "You only rented me tonight so that you could show me how to care for Matthew?"

"Yes," Kiara said enthusiastically. "This is important

stuff. And last time I was here, you mentioned that you wished I could teach you some skills."

Trey opened the binder and Kiara had to hold back a laugh at the way he was looking at it. "Uh... Thanks, I guess."

"You're welcome." Kiara glanced around the room. "May I ask... Do you keep a crib in your bedroom as well, or only your living room?"

Trey looked down at the crib. "Only here in the living room. I'm on a deadline and the crib is centrally located to my office and the kitchen."

Kiara lifted a couple of folded blankets. "So, you've just been sleeping on the couch?"

"Yes," Trey said with a laugh. "I'm guessing from that look on your face that you think I should sleep with the crib in my bedroom?"

"I didn't say that," Kiara said, dropping the blankets. "But it would probably be a better night's sleep for you and Matthew. I would actually suggest a nursery, but since you're only watching Matthew for a short while, it isn't necessary. Your bedroom is probably more relaxing and calming. It's not that your living room isn't. I just wonder if it would be more comfortable."

"Um, I guess I never thought of that."

"No worries. You can consider that more when I leave. Tonight, I figured we could go over the basics, like diapering, feeding, burping, nap schedules, the correct way to warm a bottle, ensuring you have a routine. That sort of thing."

Kiara laughed aloud when Trey dragged his long fingers down his face, glancing at the kitchen before turning back to her. "Will we at least have time to eat before we dive into all this?"

Kiara smiled. "Sure. I haven't eaten anything yet, so dinner would be nice."

Trey returned her smile. "Great. I'll go set the table." Twenty minutes later, they were seated at the table and dinner was served. Kiara was surprised to find that Trey had made filet mignon, green beans and white rice.

"You've outdone yourself," Kiara said. "This tastes way better than the takeout we had the other night."

Trey laughed. "I had to redeem myself after that dinner fiasco. I'm glad you like it."

"I do. You didn't have to make me dinner, but I appreciate it."

Trey looked up at her and held her gaze. "I have a confession to make. After that kiss we shared the other night, I assumed you'd rented me so that we could get to know one another on a more personal level. I had no idea you wanted to meet about Matthew."

"I thought about coming clean and telling you when you called me last night to confirm, but where's the fun in that?" Kiara smiled slyly.

Trey lifted his hands in surrender. "Yeah, you got me. I had a different night in mind. But I must admit, you know your stuff. I'm still trying to nail down this parenting thing, but you're going to make an amazing mother."

Kiara shifted uncomfortably in her seat. "Ah, yeah. I guess I would. But I don't want to have kids, so it's sort of a moot point."

Trey cleared his throat. "Really? Can I ask why?"

Kiara pushed her food around her plate as she prepared to give the response she normally did when she was asked that question. "I mentioned the other night that I practically had to raise my siblings on my own. Although my siblings are scattered around the LA area, each of them has kids and I absolutely love being a doting aunt and spoiling them whenever I can."

Kiara forced herself to remain still as Trey studied her some more. "What about LA Little Ones? You're so great with children."

"Just because I don't want kids of my own doesn't mean I don't love being around them. I'm great at what I do and I think my upbringing and helping to raise my siblings helped with that."

"I understand," Trey said. "Last month, I would have told you that I don't think I want to have children, either. But being around Matthew is starting to change my opinion."

Kiara's heart broke a little, even though it shouldn't have. She and Trey had just met, so why did it matter that he wanted children and she didn't? *You know why it matters. You just don't want to admit it to yourself.* If there was anything she'd learned in her past relationships, it was that a couple had to be on the same page about important life-changing decisions. If they weren't, it could ruin the relationship.

Trey leaned back in his chair and continued to observe her. After a few moments, she couldn't sit still anymore. "You know it's not polite to stare, right?"

"I'm sorry," he said. "I hope I don't offend you by what I'm about to say, but you are one of the warmest and most nurturing women I've ever met. And although we haven't known one another for long, something tells me that you'd love to be a mother and would make a great one."

Kiara glanced back down at her plate and sucked in a much-needed breath. "Thanks for the compliment, but I'm better off spending my time caring for the children of others, rather than my own."

Trey watched her for a few more seconds, then resumed eating. "Well, if it's any consolation," he said. "If you ever change your mind about having children, I think you'd make an amazing mother."

Kiara smiled, her heart breaking a little more. *How do I respond to that?* He didn't know her story. He didn't know her past. She'd barely known Trey for a week, yet when they were together, all she wanted to do was pour out her heart and soul to him.

How can I tell him my deepest, darkest fears and expect him to understand what others haven't? More important, how would she ever be able to let him go at the end of all this? No matter what happened between them, it would end. It always did. There was no way around it, and Kiara was fooling herself if she let her hopes convince her that Trey was different from the others.

"Thank you," she finally said, pushing through the tears that were lodged in the back of her throat. Trey was seeing her through rose-colored glasses, so all he saw was the good in her. The potential in her. The Kiara who was great with kids and ran her own day-care center and preschool. The Kiara who would no doubt have kids of her own because, logically, who would surround themselves each day with the one thing they didn't want?

Kiara had been around enough men to know when one was genuinely interested in the possibility of a future with her. However, when Trey found out the truth, he would leave her just like others had before him.

Kiara had rehearsed her I-never-want-to-have-kids speech more times than she could count, yet each time she said the words, it didn't get any easier. She doubted it would ever be possible to lie to someone you could see a future with by telling him that you never wanted to have kids of your own, when the hard truth was, she physically *couldn't* have kids of her own. *Her* truth wasn't the truth Trey wanted to hear, but it was her burden to bear.

Trey nodded his head to the classic R & B hit that filled the speakers of his sports car. He'd just dropped off Matthew at LA Little Ones and was headed to Prescott George's LA chapter headquarters to meet with a few members regarding an inner school program that Trey was hoping to get off the ground to help ensure that all students had a gift for the holidays.

He'd hoped to get his program running way before October, but the six-month suspension had really pushed them back. At least his screenplay was going much better than expected. He was almost finished and Trey had actually been happy when Carmen asked him if he could keep Matthew for longer. He wanted to spend all the time he could with the little dude.

As Trey neared the Fine Arts Building, his phone

rang. "Hey, Kendrick," Trey said, accepting his friend's call through his car's Bluetooth.

"Hey, Trey. Do you have a couple minutes to spare?"

"Sure. What's up?"

"I just wanted to tell you that tonight, Nicole and Kyra are hosting a congratulations party at the Bare Sophistication boutique since our production company is officially booked solid for the next twelve months with projects."

Trey smiled. He'd known Kendrick's production company would be a success. "Congrats, man. I'm happy for you. I can try and make it tonight, but I would have my nephew with me. Would that be okay?"

"That's fine," Kendrick said. "There will be a few kids there. My mom and a couple other women agreed to babysit during the party, so Matthew will be in good hands. Unless you want to carry him around like you did at the bachelor event."

Trey laughed. "I'll bring the carrier just in case. If I can make it, what time should I be there?"

"Probably around 6:00 p.m. should be fine," Kendrick said. "And it was also my job to make sure you knew that Kiara had also been invited and had confirmed she was coming."

"Oh, did she, now. In that case, I'll definitely be there."

"I figured," Kendrick said with a laugh. "How are things going between you two? Keeping it friendly or do you think there's potential for more?"

Trey thought back to last night, when Kiara had come over. She'd pulled a fast one on him by renting him to teach him how to care for Matthew versus a date like he'd originally thought, but he'd still had a good time with her. Dinner had been a little more tense than he'd liked, but after dinner, Kiara had gone through her bag of tricks. By the end of the night, they'd both discussed more about their careers and families and even laughed over some of the things Trey had done wrong since Carmen had left Matthew in his care.

"It depends," Trey said. "Are you asking man-to-man? Or are you asking for Nicole and Kyra?"

"A little bit of both," Kendrick said. "I was curious myself since the chemistry between you both was evident during the Rent-a-Bachelor event. But Nicole and Kyra also told me that I had to ask next time I talked to you. I figured that if I tell them what you say before you get here tonight, they won't bother you as much."

Trey laughed and Kendrick joined in. They both knew that wasn't true. "If you must know, I would be interested in a relationship with Kiara, but I'm not sure how she feels about it. We haven't really discussed it yet. Just playing it day by day."

"I get that," Kendrick said. "And I'm glad you're coming tonight."

"Me, too. See you then."

Once inside the Fine Arts Building, Trey took the elevator to the penthouse, his mind still on Kiara. He was almost to the meeting room when he heard his name called.

"Hey, Mr. Davis," Trey said. "It's good to see you."

"It's good to see you, too, son. I've been meaning to check on you and your brothers to see how you are doing."

Trey hoped his eyes hadn't widened at the statement. He couldn't recall anyone ever referring to him and his brothers in the same sentence. "We're doing as good as can be expected," Trey said. He'd barely finished with his statement before Demetrius Davis began talking about things Trey was less than interested in.

Demetrius was one of Reginald's best friends, and being a part of Prescott George, Trey always found it a bit awkward when any of Reginald's friends approached him as if he and his father were on the best of terms. At times, Trey almost wanted to stop them from talking to ask if they were sure they were speaking to the right son, because Max was the only one close to Reginald.

"You'll let me know then, right, Trey?"

Trey shook his head in an attempt to hide his glazed-over eyes. "Sorry. What did you say?"

"I was just saying that Reginald called and told me that you and your brothers are trying to prove his innocence. Therefore, I'd like to offer my services in any way I can. Since I'm a higher-ranking member of Prescott George, I may have access to some files and data that you don't have access to."

"That would be great," Trey said. "We have a couple leads, but nothing solid."

Demetrius glanced to his left at a young woman whom Trey had seen a few times in the LA headquarters.

"Trey, have you met my personal assistant, Christina North?"

"No, I haven't," Trey said as he outstretched his hand. "It's nice to meet you."

"Nice to meet you, Mr. Moore."

"Christina will also be able to assist you and your brothers with the investigation if you need our help."

"We appreciate it." Trey glanced over his shoulder at the meeting room. "I'll follow up with you both on how you can help after I speak with my brothers. However, right now, I hate to be rude, but I have a meeting that's about to start."

"Oh, yes," Demetrius said, waving his hands toward the room. "The inner-city holiday program meeting. I forgot. Go right ahead."

"You both have a good day."

Before he walked into the meeting room, he shot Max and Derek a quick text message about Demetrius's offer to help. Trey wasn't too fond of Reginald's friends—mainly because he wasn't too fond of Reginald himself—but at this point, they needed all the help they could get if they were going to prove Reginald's innocence.

Chapter 8

"Jackpot!" Kiara said as she parked a few stores down from Bare Sophistication and got out of her vehicle. Finding parking in LA was always a toss-up. Kiara was proud of herself for agreeing to attend a party on a weekday. Especially since she'd spent last night at Trey's, so she hadn't gotten much sleep.

If only the lack of sleep had been for a much more intimate reason. She paused on the sidewalk and shook her head. "Talk like that won't get you anywhere," she said to herself. "You can't decide to be friends with the man and then change your mind."

Kiara had never been the indecisive type, but with Trey, she wasn't confident in any decision she made about him. Friends? Not friends? More than friends? If she kept this up, she was going to drive herself crazy.

When Kiara approached the door to the boutique, she noticed the Closed sign on the door. She glanced inside and rang the doorbell, smoothing down her royal blue cocktail dress. *What if Trey is here?* As she'd learned at Rent-a-Bachelor, they seemed to know some of the same people. Kyra had called and invited her to this party to celebrate the success of her friends' production company. Kiara had met Nicole and Kendrick at the bachelor event, and now that she remembered, the couple had been talking to Trey when Kyra had dragged her over to approach them.

Please tell me he won't be here tonight. Every morning that he dropped off Matthew, Kiara managed to be conveniently unavailable. This morning had been no different. Seeing that man two days in a row had sent her lady parts into a frenzy, so the less Trey time she had, the better.

It didn't take long for Kyra to reach the door. "Hey, Kiara," Kyra said, welcoming her into the party. "So glad you could make it."

"Thanks for inviting me." Kiara handed her a bottle of wine. "Where is everyone?"

"We closed the store early, but the party is upstairs in the loft. Nothing major. Only about twenty people or so. Nicole and Kendrick plan on having something bigger after the holidays."

"Well, considering my idea of a party has been Netflix and a glass of wine, I'd say twenty people is a lot," she said with a laugh. *And if Trey is in that twenty, then that's not nearly enough people to distract me from him.* It was on the tip of her tongue to ask, but she didn't.

Kyra led her to the stairs. "You've never been to our boudoir studio, right?"

"Nope, I've only been in the boutique part."

"That's what I thought. We turned the loft into our studio and it's much more spacious up there. I'll introduce you to some folks and give you a tour." When they reached the top of the stairs, Nicole came over to greet Kiara.

"Thanks for coming, Kiara." Kiara returned Nicole's hug.

"Thanks for having me." She handed Nicole a card. "Congrats on all your success."

Kiara glanced around the room, noticing that it appeared to be more than twenty people there. More like thirty plus. Luckily, she didn't see Trey.

"How about I show you around first," Kyra said. She motioned around the spacious main room that served as the boudoir lounge. She took Kiara to the makeup and hair station, which was Nicole's domain when she wasn't working at the business she and her husband had opened. Then Kyra led her to two different rooms that had a variety of boudoir props, including a beautiful Victorian-style bed and a plush chaise lounge. The parlor and powder room walls adorned with black-and-white boudoir photos were Kiara's favorite.

"Everything is beautiful," she said as they walked back to the main room. "I can see why you've been so successful."

"Thanks! I really enjoy managing Bare Sophistication. We try to make this space one that would allow a woman to be herself and feel comfortable. Come on. I'll introduce you to a few people."

"Sure," Kiara said, turning to follow Kyra to a group of people standing in the corner. As they approached the group, movement in the corner of Kiara's eye caught her attention. She turned to her left, noticing a large balcony for the first time. The sight on the balcony made her pause.

"Oh," Kyra said, noticing that she'd stopped. "Did I forget to tell you that Trey is here?"

Kiara glanced at Kyra. "Yeah, friend. You sort of forgot to tell me that. And you conveniently didn't give me a tour of the balcony where he is currently standing."

Kyra shrugged. "I hadn't gotten that far yet. Why? Is there an issue with Trey being here?"

Kiara sighed, deciding to be honest. "I never know how to act around that man. Do I avoid him? Keep things friendly? Push for more? And then that kiss…"

"Wait a minute!" Kyra said, a little louder than Kiara would have liked. "You and Trey kissed?"

"Yeah." Kiara scanned the room. "Why don't you say it a little louder. I don't think he heard you on the balcony."

"Sorry." Kyra dropped her voice lower. "You guys kissed? When? Where? How was it? How was he? Did you like it? Did he like it?"

Kiara's eyes widened as she tried to answer. "Yes. A day after we met. At his home. It was amazing. He was amazing. I liked it. And I'm pretty sure he liked it."

Kyra frowned. "Liked it? You liked it and you think he just liked it? Not loved it or any other word that would better describe a kiss with a man like that?" Kiara followed Kyra's outreached hand that pointed toward the balcony. She wasn't sure if Trey sensed she was there or if he just happened to glance back into the loft, but their eyes collided before she could catch her next breath.

As it always did, his intense gaze froze her in her spot. *You'd think I'd be used to those almost-black eyes by now.* It didn't matter how many times she saw him, or how frequently she saw him, that look in his eyes still caught her off guard.

He nodded in her direction, and in return, she smiled back. When his appreciative eyes openly looked her up and down before meeting her eyes again, she shuffled from one foot to the other.

"Do you want to tell me the truth now?" Kyra asked, regaining her attention. Kiara kept her eyes focused on Trey as she spoke.

"I loved the kiss, probably more than I should." Kiara's eyes dropped to his lips. "And I'm pretty sure he enjoyed it just as much." She finally turned to face Kyra. "I was thinking we could keep things friendly between us, but I'm not sure Trey and I even know how to do friendly. True, we're building a friendship. But *platonic* isn't exactly the word that comes to mind when we get together."

"I already knew it would be like this," Kyra said. "The way you both were staring at each other from across the room the first time you met was a dead giveaway. The only thing I don't understand is why you're trying to keep things platonic between you and Trey. Girl, have you looked at that man? Every woman at that bachelor event was trying to get in his pants, but he only had eyes for you."

Kiara looked back in Trey's direction only to find him still staring at her. She recognized the man that was on the balcony with him as Nicole's husband, Kendrick. In her peripheral vision, she noticed Kyra wave her hand at Kendrick, and seconds later, he stepped back into the loft, leaving Trey alone on the balcony.

"What are you doing?" Kiara asked.

Kyra lifted an eyebrow. "Helping you out, girlfriend, because clearly, the two of you would stand here and stare at each other all night. Now that Kendrick is back inside, you'll have privacy. So, go out there and greet your man." Kyra gave her a nudge, pushing her closer to the door that led to the balcony.

Kiara had probably walked only a few steps, but it felt like much longer as she made her way to where Trey stood, still watching her.

Just breathe, she said to herself when her hand touched the handle. *You've spent plenty of alone time with him. As a matter of fact, you just saw him last night. Having a casual conversation is fine. Just be yourself.*

Her pep talk sounded easy in theory, but once she stepped onto the balcony and felt the door close behind her, she forgot everything she'd convinced herself to do.

Trey smiled. "You look beautiful, as always."

"Thank you," she said breathlessly. "You look handsome as well. How long have you been here?"

"Only about an hour."

She looked around the spacious balcony. "Where is Matthew?"

"He's with Kendrick's mom. She's watching a few other kids as well."

Kiara nodded. "That's nice of her."

"It is."

The balcony grew quiet again. *Come on, Kiara! Say something!* The sexual tension was so strong she could barely focus on anything else. She couldn't place what made tonight feel different from other times they'd spent together, but everything felt more heightened. Intensified.

The sun was setting behind him, casting a glow around him and forcing her to centralize her gaze on him even more than she already was. He was sporting all black, and whatever cologne he was wearing was causing her hypersensitive nipples to harden. His eyes briefly dropped to her chest, apparently noticing the change. Had she not been watching him so intently, she would have missed his quick perusal.

Trey glanced to the corner of the balcony before stepping closer to her. He seemed to glide across the floor and she didn't stop him when his arms curled around her waist and guided her to the corner away from the party.

She leaned against the wall, more aware of him now than she'd ever been. He glanced down at her, the back of his hand caressing her cheek while the other hand kept her pulled close. When his lips hovered over hers, he kept his eyes locked on her. She arched her back off the wall, which brought her body closer to his. He moaned when her hardened nipples made contact with his chest.

"Sweet Kiara," he said. His voice was low and deep. She expected him to kiss her, but instead, he continued to observe her through lidded eyes.

Please, the voice inside her begged. *Just kiss me already!* She knew what she'd said before about keeping things platonic, but now she realized that there was no way that would be possible. The words *Trey* and *platonic* didn't even belong in the same sentence.

Trey sucked in a breath and pushed a piece of hair from her face. She knew he wanted to kiss her. All the signs were there. And she sure as heck wanted to kiss him.

"Trey," she said, placing her hands on his chest. She'd had every intention of initiating the kiss, but she didn't have to. Trey dropped his lips to hers, lightly suckling her bottom lip, before claiming her entire mouth. She moaned when the hand on her waist moved to her backside and pulled her closer to the fit of him.

Her hands went to the back of his neck, pulling him closer. Needing more, she lifted one of her legs and was grateful when Trey caught her thigh in his free hand. Kiara wasted no time giving him entry into her mouth, and unlike last time, Trey didn't stop the kiss when their tongues passionately danced to the soft sounds of the wind and background noise.

Every part of Kiara was on fire, and judging by the groans coming from Trey, he was just as wrapped up in the kiss as she was. A few minutes later, the kiss ended, leaving them both winded and Kiara craving more.

"I had to do that," Trey said, helping her back to the floor of the balcony. "I couldn't believe I let you leave last night without kissing you."

Kiara laughed. "I needed it, too." She looked back toward the party. "Should we go back inside?"

Trey looked in that same direction before looking down at his pants. "How about we stay out here a little longer?"

Kiara glanced down at the bulge threatening to burst through the zipper of his pants. "Okay, we can." They walked over to the blanket and two chairs that sat overlooking the LA streets and nightlife.

They sat in comfortable silence for a few moments, each wrapped up in their own thoughts.

"I meant to ask you last night," Kiara said, breaking the silence. "How are things going with Reginald and the investigation to prove his innocence?"

"It's coming along," Trey said. "For the first time this past weekend, my brothers and I all gathered at Reginald's home. We haven't found any information to aid in his claim yet, but getting to know my half brothers has been the best part so far."

Kiara smiled. "That must be nice. To finally relate to each other after all this time."

"It is, but in a way, I wish we had tried to have a relationship earlier. To be brought together under the circumstances and with Reginald so sick is disheartening."

"What do you mean *sick*?"

Trey shifted in his chair. "Reginald told us he has prostate cancer and was only given a few months to live. Hence the newfound desire to bring his sons together and apologize for never being a father to me and my brother Derek."

"I'm so sorry to hear that," she said, lightly touching Trey's arm. "And I hope you and your brothers get the answers you're looking for."

"Thank you," he said, placing his hand on top of hers. "I'm not sure he's innocent, but while I was at his home, I realized how much I hope that he's telling the truth."

"There's nothing wrong with holding on to hope," Kiara said.

Trey let out a forced laugh. "It is when the man in question is Reginald. For a while, I never even referred to him as Reginald. I used to refer to him as *the cheater*. It wasn't a clever nickname, but as a young boy, I couldn't think of anything else to call the man who cheated on my mom with my brother Derek's mom, then dropped his mom for Max's mom, subsequently forgetting he even had two other sons."

"I can't imagine how that must have felt," Kiara said in a soft voice. "I guess I can see why that would give you mixed feelings about feeling hopeful that he's innocent."

Trey nodded. "It really does. Max has always been close to him, so I also feel bad for my brother. He didn't grow up with the Reginald that Derek and I knew, so while I may feel an unexplained loss when Reginald dies, Max will feel that loss a whole lot more."

Kiara nodded in agreement. "I understand that. However, you also can't discount your feelings just because they are different than Max's. Yes, Max will grieve for the father he's always known. But you are allowed to grieve for the father you've never had. Take it from someone who was more on Max's side of things. Since I'm the oldest, my siblings didn't have the type of close relationship with my dad like I did. Yet they still suffered a great loss because not only did he leave us, but they never even really knew him like I did. I had to understand their loss just as they had to understand mine."

Kiara glanced down at the well-lit LA street that was bustling with people going out for the night.

"I'm sure it was extremely hard," Trey said. "Growing up so fast and having to help raise siblings when you were heartbroken over the absence of your father?"

"It was." Kiara sighed. "I will always be the first to tell you that my mom is superwoman. Raising four children and working two jobs was not easy, yet that woman did everything without complaining. Growing up, I admired her so much that I never understood how my dad could leave such a sweet woman. Now my mom is finally traveling the world and doing things she always wanted to do. But even today, I have to remind her not to worry about us and to focus on herself."

"Good luck with that," Trey said with a laugh. "A mother's job is to worry about her kids. Right now, my mom and stepdad are on an African safari, but it took my sister, Carmen, months while she was pregnant to convince my mom that it was okay for them to travel even though M-dog is so young. I think my mom was afraid of me being my sister's main support with M-dog if they were gone for a while."

"I know I tease you about taking care of Matthew, but you really are doing a good job. You can tell he's happy spending so much time with you." Kiara sat straighter in her chair. "You know what? I don't think I ever asked how you ended up babysitting Matthew for so long."

"My sister, Carmen, got a minor role on a television pilot and she needed to film for two weeks. She recently called and asked me if she could extend M-dog's stay for an additional couple days, and of course, I said yes."

"That's so awesome," Kiara said. "So your sister is an actress like your mom is?"

"An aspiring one, yes. She got the acting chops. I got the writing chops."

As Trey continued to talk about his family, Kiara observed the proud look on his face and the way his eyes shone with pride. Halfway through their conversation, the door to the balcony opened.

"Um, hello?" Kyra said. "Are you both going to sit out here and talk all night, or are you actually going to socialize with the rest of us?"

Kiara laughed. "We were just about to come in. Just soaking in this great LA view."

"Oh, okay." Kyra looked from Trey to Kiara. "Because for a minute, I thought you both were about to hide in the corner again to make out and do God knows what else."

Kiara shook her head. "Kyra!"

"What," Kyra said with a shrug. "None of us blame you two for wanting to get your freak on when you see each other because, *dayum*, the looks you two give one another are hot enough to light us all on fire. But the party is inside, so how about you set up a date to sex each other's brains out when we aren't all eavesdropping on your private time." With that, Kyra walked away from the door she'd conveniently left open.

"Sorry about that," Kiara said. "She literally has no filter."

Trey laughed. "She doesn't bother me. Her bluntness

is refreshing." Trey stood from his chair and reached out his hand to assist Kiara. Once their hands touched, Kiara felt tingles throughout her entire body. *I hope that feeling never goes away*, she thought despite herself. *I can't imagine not feeling this each time we touch.*

"It won't," Trey said, his eyes capturing hers in a penetrating hold. "And neither do I."

"Did I just say that out loud?" Kiara asked. "Please tell me I didn't."

Trey shook his head and laughed. "Wish I could tell you what you want to hear, but you definitely said that out loud." He stepped closer to her. "I'm starting to realize that, sometimes, you say out loud what you're thinking, but you don't realize it unless I respond to your so-called thought."

Kiara lightly slapped her forehead. "And the award for most embarrassing moment of the night goes to… yours truly."

Kiara was prepared for Trey to shoot her back a sarcastic comment. Or maybe even a comforting one. Yet he didn't do either. Instead, he pulled her in for another toe-curling kiss, although this time, people at the party could see them.

Kiara kept her hands to her sides, assuming the catcalls from inside the loft would cause Trey to stop the dancing of their mouths, but they didn't. When their kiss deepened and her hands went around his neck, Kiara had no choice but to soak in every bit of passion Trey Moore was offering.

Chapter 9

Trey walked into Lou's Diner and immediately spotted his brothers at a table in the corner.

"Hey, fellas," he said when he approached. "Did you order yet?"

"Yes," Derek said. "We ordered you the same thing we had at your place during our first meeting."

"Thanks." Trey pulled up a seat in between Derek and Max, who were sitting across from each other. "Did you get my message yesterday about Demetrius offering to help?"

"Yes, we were just discussing that," Derek said. "You and Max know Demetrius more than I do. Do either of you really think he can help?"

"I'm not sure," Trey said. "But right now, I think we need the help."

"I agree. We need the help," Max said. "Trey, has your contact gotten any further along on figuring out who may have hacked into the files?"

"Actually, he did." Trey pulled out a small notepad. "Pete was able to track down the fact that the hacker is from a small contractor group from the dark web who call themselves Insenia."

"Is he able to get the names of everyone in Insenia?" Derek asked.

"No one has ever been able to track how many are in this group, but word is there are no more than ten hackers. He won't be able to tell me their actual names, but now that he knows Insenia is involved, he's going to see if he's able to follow the crumbs and gain access to chat with one of the members through the dark web."

Max nodded. "So basically, we'd contact them and pretend as if we're interested in hiring them ourselves?"

"Exactly," Trey said. "I also have Pete investigating the security footage of the break-ins at the San Diego headquarters since he now has access to their server. He's looking to see if anything was doctored since Reginald was placed at the scene during the time the historic artifacts were stolen."

"That's good," Max said. "If he was framed for this, hopefully the real culprit wasn't able to cover his tracks like he thought."

"Looks like we're getting somewhere," Derek said. "One way or another, I want the truth."

Trey and Max nodded in agreement. "I also wonder if maybe someone from the San Diego chapter is behind this," Trey said. "We've been so busy looking into someone from LA trying to frame Reginald, but Reginald has enemies everywhere."

"I've thought about that, too," Max said. "Reginald has been a high-ranking board member for twenty-five years, and in that time, he's rubbed a lot of people the wrong way. He's been longtime rivals with some of the San Diego members, so I could see one of them being behind the frame-up."

Trey looked to Derek. "I know being an active member of Prescott George has never been your thing, but we could really use your keen eye at a few of these events. I'm thinking that all three of us need to show a united Moore partnership to get to the bottom of this."

Derek remained quiet.

"I agree with Trey," Max said. "Besides, Trey and I have more of a relationship with the members and I wonder if we're too close to the situation at times. You have a fresh set of eyes and we think you'll be able to spot any bs."

Derek smiled and nodded. "Okay, I'll attend more events until we solve this case. I want the truth, so I understand I have to do my part as well."

When the food arrived, the brothers ate for a while in silence, letting all the information from the investigation soak in.

"This place is still as good as I remember," Derek said after a few moments.

"It is." Trey took a bite of bacon. "Although things are going well, I'm so busy finalizing the end of my screenplay and watching M-dog, I feel like I haven't been eating consistently."

"I get like that every time I'm busy," Derek said. "How is M-dog doing?"

Trey smiled. "He's doing good. Every morning I drop him off at LA Little Ones and pick him up in the evening, so he's with me at night."

"I've heard of that place," Max said. "It's owned by Kiara Woods, right?"

"Yeah, it is." Trey raised a questioning eyebrow. "Do you know her?"

"Not like that, bro. Calm down." Max laughed as he placed his hands in front of him. "I've never actually met her. I just read about the success of her business in the newspaper last year. That's all. I'm assuming, from that look you're giving me and your accusatory tone, you're feeling her?"

"Damn right," Trey said, not hiding how he felt for Kiara. "I met her the night of the Rent-a-Bachelor kickoff, and she took pity on me and allowed me to register M-dog for LA Little Ones for a couple weeks until Carmen picks him up."

"And you've been dating her?" Derek asked.

"Trying to," Trey said with a laugh. "She told me she isn't interested in a relationship and I get the feeling she wants to focus on her business right now."

Max shook his head. "Then I suggest you listen, bro."

"Me, too," Derek said. "When a woman tells you something, you better listen. Otherwise, you'll never hear the end of it."

"I hear what y'all are saying, but Kiara is giving me mixed signals. One minute she's keeping me at a friendly distance, and the next minute she's kissing me more passionately than any woman has ever kissed me before."

"So, you like her more than you're letting on?" Max asked.

"Much more." Trey leaned back in his chair, thinking about last night with Kiara. Had they not been at a party, he could have stayed out there on that balcony talking to her all night. Anytime he was with her, he didn't want their time together to end.

"Back when I was in high school, a girl I liked broke my heart when she told me I was too deep for her. I think it had something to do with the types of letters I used to write her between classes. I couldn't help but be poetic, even back then," Trey said and then recalled another experience.

"In college, I had a couple of serious relationships with women who understood me and my love for words, so I thought I was finally around more like-minded people. But even then, I found that to be exhausting at times. I didn't fit in with the literature buffs, nor did I fit in with the spoken-word lovers. That's when I went on a search for my own crowd of people."

"Cute story, sunshine," Derek teased.

"Is there a reason you're getting sentimental on us, bro?" Max asked.

Trey clasped his hands in front of him, surprised he was sharing so much. "When I discovered screenwriting, it felt as if all the pieces of my life finally fit together in a puzzle. It didn't matter that I'd grown up without Reginald in my life. It may sound harsh, but it didn't even matter at the time that I wasn't as close to my brothers as I wanted to be. Writing screenplays gave me purpose, and the television and film lovers—whom coincidentally I'd been around my entire life thanks to my mom—turned out to be like family. They filled those voids that had been left open. However, over the years, writing screenplays has felt more like an annoying job at times, rather than fulfilling a dream like it used to be. I haven't felt fulfilled in a long time, yet being around Kiara, I feel alive again. I may have only known her for a short amount of time, but I'm falling hard, fellas."

Derek and Max shared a look of understanding. "I take back my statement," Derek said. "In this case, maybe you should go after what you want. Especially since Kiara is obviously what you want. It's possible she said she wasn't interested because she's so used to her routine and M-dog gives both of you an excuse to keep each other at a certain distance. Or maybe she was even hurt in the past. So, my suggestion is that you take her away for a weekend outside of LA. Someplace where you both can explore the possibility of something more."

"I can't go anywhere now," Trey said. "I'll be finished editing my screenplay by tonight, but we have the investigation going on and we all need to see this through."

"Derek's right," Max said. "You shared Pete's contact info with us when we started this investigation, but we've been letting you spearhead it. We can handle the investigation while you're gone."

"And we can take turns dropping M-dog off at LA

Little Ones," Derek added. "You'll only be gone the weekend, so we'd only be watching him a couple nights."

Trey looked from Derek to Max, stunned that his brothers would offer to do this for him given that they'd just started building a relationship.

"I don't know what to say," Trey said. "I'm grateful that you both would do this for me."

"You can thank us by taking this woman you're falling for someplace special this weekend," Derek said. "Do you already have someplace in mind?"

"Hopefully someplace that will blow her mind away," Max chimed in. "If you're trying to win her heart, you have to really go for it. And what's the point of having money if we can't spoil the women we care about?"

Trey smiled slyly. He didn't even have to give the destination a second thought. "I know exactly where to take Kiara on a weekend vacation. And if I have my way, by the end of the trip, she'll know exactly how I feel."

Chapter 10

"Over here, Kiara!"

Kiara looked through the crowd in the busy café and spotted her friend Kyra sitting at a table in the far corner.

"Thank you so much for meeting me for lunch," Kiara said as she bent down to hug Kyra. "I am in desperate need of some advice." With Miranda still in Dubai, Kiara was grateful to have a friend in Kyra.

"I figured," Kyra said with a laugh. "I know this week was busy for you at LA Little Ones, and typically, when you're busy I don't even see you. But thankfully, I'm seeing you twice in one week. I ordered some soup and sandwiches for us. Is that okay?"

"That's perfect." Kiara placed her purse next to her on the table. "I'm freaking out a bit."

"Oh, no. Is it about Trey?" Kyra asked. "Is everything okay?"

Kiara sighed. "Everything's fine... Unless you take into consideration that he called me late last night and asked if I would spend a weekend away with him."

Kyra clapped her hands. "That's awesome."

"We would leave tomorrow."

Kyra's eyes widened. "Wow, that's soon! But it's still awesome, though. Waiting for the problem." Kyra took a sip of her water.

Kiara crossed her arms over her chest. "Weekend vacation. Leaving tomorrow. Traveling via private jet. Headed to the French Riviera!"

Kyra almost spit her water out across the table. "Say what? He's jet-setting you to Europe for a weekend vacation?"

"Yup." Kiara ran her fingers down her face, careful not to mess up her makeup. "He's waiting for my answer if I'm going or not. He needs to know soon, hence our emergency lunch date. Honestly, it was so late last night that I almost thought I'd dreamed the entire thing. Then he texted me a few hours ago about my decision and I realized it wasn't a dream after all."

"I beg to differ," Kyra said, shaking her head. "A fine-ass Millionaire Mogul calls you in the middle of the night and asks if he can take you away for a weekend in one of the most romantic places in the world... I'd say that was pretty dreamy."

"This is insane, though, right? I mean, I can't possibly go with him on such short notice."

Kyra squinted her eyes. "Could your business afford to have you gone?"

"Yes." Kiara had already checked with her nursery director and activities director just in case. "They actually encouraged me to go."

"Then could you be packed by tomorrow?"

"Yes."

"Do you want to have Trey all to yourself this weekend?"

"More than anything."

"Could you be falling for him?"

Kiara sighed. "Yeah, I think I am."

Kyra waved her hands in the air. "Then what exactly is the problem, girlfriend? Opportunities like this don't come around often and I saw you two together in the loft this week. He's so into you and some of my friends were saying that you seemed like a couple that's been together for a long time."

"That's how I feel when I'm with him," Kiara said. "We just met, yet he understands me more than any man I've ever met. Which is so strange because there is still so much more of me that he still doesn't know."

"That's why you need this weekend together." Kyra placed her hand on Kiara's shoulder. "We weren't friends when you were married, and I wasn't there for your divorce, either. But in the year I've known you, I've never seen you look as happy as you do when you're with Trey. You've claimed to not want a relationship, but you have to realize that as cliché as it sounds, love finds us when we least expect it."

Kiara leaned back in her chair, letting Kyra's words

sink in. "I know you're right, and I think that's part of the problem. Some of the things that Trey doesn't know about me are definite relationship deal breakers. On one hand, I can't believe that I'm starting to fall for him so fast. We've only shared a couple kisses, and yet in those kisses, I feel like he sees into my soul. Like his mouth is coaxing me to open my heart to him and bare secrets that I promised to take to my grave. My gut is telling me to accept his invitation and spend the weekend away with him. But my heart is telling me to tread carefully and keep myself guarded."

"Psssh." Kyra swatted her hand in the air. "I never listen to the voice that tells me to slow down. Only the one that flashes *Keep moving at rapid speed* in bright neon colors. I think you need to mute that indecisive voice in your head and listen to your inner daredevil."

"What if the voice I mute is the voice of reason?"

Kyra shrugged. "What if the voice of reason is also the voice that will doom you to a lifetime of unhappiness, no love, terrible sex and bad hair days?"

Kiara laughed. "There's no in-between with you, is there? It's all or nothing."

"Duh!" Kyra joined her in her laughter. "Kiara, you already know this about me! You didn't ask me to lunch so that I could tell you to back away from the cliff. You wanted to talk to me so that I could drag you to the edge and throw your ass off it."

By the time their food arrived, Kiara was laughing so hard her stomach hurt. "Okay," Kiara said. "I'm going to tell him I can go on the trip."

"So happy you made the right decision because you know what this means, right?"

Kiara took a sip of soup. "I'm almost afraid to ask, but I will. What does it mean?"

Kyra rubbed her hands together sneakily. "It means after we eat lunch, you're taking another hour to come with me back to Bare Sophistication. It's time to clear out those cobwebs and buy you some sexy lingerie that's guaranteed to get you laid."

Kiara frowned. "What makes you think I haven't been laid in a while?"

"Girl, please. You're more high-strung than a guitar that's been wound up too tight. Don't think I didn't see your freaky tail lift your leg and wrap it around Trey's waist when you were kissing on the balcony the other day."

Kiara gasped. "You saw that? Why were you looking?"

"Um, hello! Lots of folks were looking. It's windows everywhere in the boudoir studio to allow for good natural lighting for the photos. Y'all were having a pretty heavy make-out session and we weren't trying to look, but it was hard not to. Our conversations were interesting, but you and Trey were way more entertaining."

Kiara laughed. There was no point in being embarrassed. That kiss with Trey on the balcony had been mouthwatering, so she could imagine they'd put on a good show.

"Let's hurry up and eat," Kyra said, finishing up her soup and moving on to her sandwich. "First lingerie outfit is on me."

"FAST FIVE" READER SURVEY

Your participation entitles you to:
✳ **4 Thank-You Gifts Worth Over $20!**

Complete the survey in minutes.

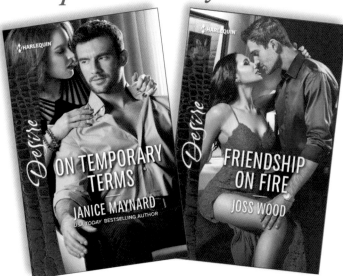

Get **2 FREE** Books

Your Thank-You Gifts include **2 FREE BOOKS** and **2 MYSTERY GIFTS**. There's no obligation to purchase anything!

See inside for details.

Dear Reader,

Since you are a lover of our books, your opinions are important to us... and so is your time.

That's why we made sure your **"FAST FIVE" READER SURVEY** can be completed in just a few minutes. Your answers to the five questions will help us remain at the forefront of women's fiction.

And, as a thank-you for participating, we'd like to send you **4 FREE THANK-YOU GIFTS!**

Enjoy your gifts with our appreciation,

Pam Powers

To get your
4 FREE THANK-YOU GIFTS:

✱ Quickly complete the "Fast Five" Reader Survey
and return the insert.

"FAST FIVE" READER SURVEY

1 Do you sometimes read a book a second or third time? ○ Yes ○ No

2 Do you often choose reading over other forms of entertainment such as television? ○ Yes ○ No

3 When you were a child, did someone regularly read aloud to you? ○ Yes ○ No

4 Do you sometimes take a book with you when you travel outside the home? ○ Yes ○ No

5 In addition to books, do you regularly read newspapers and magazines? ○ Yes ○ No

YES! I have completed the above Reader Survey. Please send me my 4 FREE GIFTS (gifts worth over $20 retail). I understand that I am under no obligation to buy anything, as explained on the back of this card.

225/326 HDL GM3T

FIRST NAME	LAST NAME

ADDRESS

APT.#   CITY

STATE/PROV.   ZIP/POSTAL CODE

READER SERVICE—Here's how it works:

* * *

Kiara glanced around her bedroom, making sure she hadn't forgotten to pack anything. Trey was picking her up in thirty minutes and she was still a nervous wreck.

The mini shopping trip with Kyra had helped calm her nerves. However, from the moment she woke up this morning, she couldn't seem to slow down her heartbeat.

When her phone rang, she thought about ignoring the call, but noticed it was her mom.

"Hey, Mom. How are you?"

"I'm doing good, sweetie. I'm still in Seattle, but I was calling because your sister told me you were going out of town this weekend."

Kiara had sent her siblings a message that she was going out of town in case they were looking for her. She'd known her brothers wouldn't ask for any details, but her sister had bugged her enough until she'd finally told her about Trey. Her mom, Gina, was currently in Seattle with a guy she'd been dating. Kiara and her siblings really liked their mother's boyfriend, Brad, and it was nice to see her happy. Kiara wasn't originally going to tell her mom she was going away for the weekend because she wanted to avoid additional questions, but she should have known her sister would blab.

"Yes, Mom. I'm going out of town, but I won't be gone long. I'll be back on Monday."

"Are you really going to the French Riviera with a man you barely know?"

Goodness, sis. Did you tell her everything? "Yes, Mom. I am. His name is Trey and his nephew goes to

LA Little Ones." She didn't want to tell her mom how they'd actually first met just recently.

"Wow, sweetie. I am surprised to hear this. But I'm happy that you're taking some time to enjoy life. You work too hard and I was worried that after you divorced Jerry, you'd never love another man again."

"Mom, I didn't say I love Trey."

"But you didn't *not* say it, either." Leave it to her mom to never miss anything.

Kiara sighed. "Are you having fun in Seattle?"

"We're having a fantastic time," Gina said. "Brad's family is so sweet, and his kids love my cooking. I've cooked every day since I've been here."

"That's great, Mom. I look forward to meeting his kids one day." Kiara and her siblings had always told their mom she should open her own café one day since she was such a good cook. Now that Gina was retired, Kiara hoped her mother would follow her dream.

"They are looking forward to meeting my kids as well. But back to you and Trey. Is it serious?"

"I'm not sure yet," she said honestly. "It feels like it is, but we still have a lot we need to discuss and learn about each other."

"Does he know you can't have children?"

Always so blunt. "He knows I don't want children. That's all. And he knows I'm divorced, but I haven't given him any details yet."

"I see," Gina said. "Kiara, I want you to enjoy yourself this weekend, but I also don't want you to ever be afraid to tell a man how you feel. Sweetie, your story is your own testimony and you wouldn't be the fierce and fearless woman you are today had you not had to face certain obstacles. If Trey cares about you, he'll understand and love you regardless."

Kiara sat on her bed and blinked back tears. "I know, Mom. I know. I'm just... I don't want... I don't know." She couldn't even get the words out.

"I know, sweetie," Gina said. "You don't want him to walk out of your life like other men before him. You want to be honest, but you're afraid of losing him before you've even really had him."

Kiara sighed. "Yes, that's exactly it."

"Kiara, everyone is afraid of something, but I didn't raise you to back away from your fears. You are a strong, successful and beautiful woman who will make a man extremely happy one day. If that man is Trey and it's meant to be, it will."

"Thanks, Mom," Kiara said with a smile. "I love you and appreciate the advice. In case I haven't said it lately, thank you for always being in my corner."

"Oh, you never have to doubt that I'll be in your corner, baby. And I'll always give you advice, even if you don't want it." Gina's laugh filled the line. "Now that I've gotten a chance to talk to you about your weekend plans, can you please explain to me what your youngest brother, Paul, meant by his message that he texted to us in the family group? He and Bianca already have two kids together out of wedlock. Are they really pregnant with a third? And did they really think it was best to tell us in a text?"

"Yes, Mom," Kiara said with a laugh. "Paul and Bianca are pregnant again and they've already told you that they don't believe in marriage, so I'm not sure you'll ever get your wedding from those two. And in case you haven't noticed, as sweet as you are, your sons are terrified to tell you news they think will make you unhappy. So that's probably why Paul texted."

"I'm excited about my grandchild," Gina said. "However, I just don't understand your brothers sometimes. At least Terrance was married before he and Angie had another kid together. And your sister is married now, so Monique and Jarrett are settled. Sometimes, I wonder if Paul and Bianca are refusing to get married only because they know I want them to. I've been gone for a month, and already, I need to come home and have a stern talk with those kids."

Kiara and Gina talked for ten more minutes and Kiara was still laughing after she'd hung up with her mom. Her mom wasn't strict about a lot of things, but being married before having kids was something she'd always enforced in them. She thought that her mom would have dropped that wish once she realized that three of her four kids hadn't listened, but it didn't matter how many kids they had before marriage—Gina was still going to push for Holy Matrimony.

When her doorbell rang, Kiara did a silent thanks to her mom for helping with her nerves. The minute Kiara opened the front door, some of her nervousness came back at the sight of Trey standing at her door casually in blue jeans and a navy blue T-shirt, but she willed the nerves away.

Coincidentally, she'd chosen to wear her blue-and-white-striped flowy dress, so their outfits matched.

"Hey, Trey. Come on in." She moved aside to let him

pass. When he turned back around to face her, she eased her hands over his shoulders and stood on her tiptoes and kissed him the way she'd been thinking about all morning. His hands immediately went around her waist, pulling her closer.

This is what I needed. This is what I've been waiting on. It was kind of ironic that the reason Kiara was so nervous was Trey, and yet the person she knew could ease her nerves was also Trey. After a few breathless moments, they ended the kiss.

"Well, good morning to you, too," Trey said, lightly pecking her nose. "Should I even ask what I did to deserve such a warm welcome?"

"I just needed to do that," she said, using the same words on him that he'd used on her the night on the balcony. "Did you want a quick tour before we leave?"

"Sure," Trey said. "It's my jet, so they'll wait for me to get there."

"Come on, sugar daddy," Kiara joked, pulling his arm. "Now it's time for you to see my home."

Between the call with her mom and the kiss with Trey, Kiara was finally able to ease most of her anxiety and focus on the weekend. She had no idea what was in store for her, but she was ready to take a page out of Kyra's book and take on the weekend at full speed.

Chapter 11

Breathe in. Breathe out. Breathe in. Breathe out. Kiara continued to chant the same words repeatedly in her head. She'd never been a good flier, but she'd always managed to get through flights without having a panic attack. *Well, except for that one time in college.*

She'd taken a sleeping pill before she and Trey had left the house, so she'd slept for the first six hours of the flight. However, now that she was awake, her anxiety about flying was starting to creep back in, and she still had at least five more hours to go.

"Are you okay?" Trey asked.

Kiara glanced at him as her hands continued to clench the arms of the seat. "Is now a good time to tell you I sort of have a fear of heights? I can't believe we still have five hours to go."

Trey looked at her bashfully. "Is now a good time to tell you that we had to refuel, so it's actually six hours left?"

"What? Please tell me you're joking."

"Wish I was, but I'm not. We actually just got back in the air twenty minutes ago. You looked so peaceful sleeping, I didn't want to wake you."

Six hours? "I think I need to pop another pill to survive this flight." She opened her purse, grabbed her bottled water and swallowed another sleeping pill.

"There's a bedroom in the back of the plane," Trey said. "Even though these seats recline, maybe you'll sleep better there than in the main cabin."

"Okay," she said, nodding. "I'll try and sleep in the bedroom."

Trey unbuckled his seat belt and motioned for her to do the same. "I'd planned on giving you a tour before we left, but you looked sleepy, so I figured I'd let you rest."

"Sorry about that," she said. "I took a sleeping pill before we left my house."

"You can get a tour after we land. I'll just show you the bedroom." Trey informed the flight attendant that he'd be right back and led Kiara to the back of the jet.

"I really wish I wasn't afraid of heights," she said, briefly glancing at the vintage wooden decor of the interior. "Your jet is beautiful."

"Thanks," Trey said. "After I made my first few million, it was one of my first major purchases."

"First few million?" Kiara lifted an eyebrow. "Just how much are you worth?" She knew people in the movie industry made money, but she hadn't thought it was that much.

Trey stopped in front of the door and glanced back at her before he opened it. Once he did, she could see why he'd worn a proud smile. In the middle of the room sat a large king-size bed and matching nightstands, with two plush chairs in each corner. On one side of the room was a large circular glass window, and on the other side was a bathroom that was larger than some hotel bathrooms.

"This is beautiful," Kiara said as she continued to admire the bedroom. "I'm surprised you don't live here as opposed to your home."

"When I first purchased this jet, I lived on it for a couple months and traveled to different areas of the world. My sister and my mom even joined me for part of that trip."

Trey leaned against the molding of the door and crossed his arms over his chest. He looked so sexy in that moment, Kiara was surprised she even understood what he was saying.

"To answer your question," Trey said. "I've never been the type to boast about how much I make. I may have come from a family of money, but I sold my first Hollywood script before I hit the age of twenty-two. I made my first million on another screenplay before age twenty-five. At age twenty-six, two of my movies were nominated for prestigious awards. One of my movies won. At twenty-eight, I'd been ranked one of the top ten screenwriters in Hollywood that year. And by age thirty, I was finally asked to write a screenplay on a comic book superhero, which had always been a dream of mine."

Kiara's mouth slightly parted. *Why the heck didn't you ever google him?* She sat on the bed, her legs suddenly wobbly. Money had never impressed her. Money couldn't buy you a good personality or a caring heart. Money couldn't comfort you after a bad day the way a pair of masculine arms could hold you. To be cliché, money couldn't buy you happiness. However, on Trey, money looked damn sexy and she'd be lying to herself if she didn't admit that his success was a major turn-on.

"I'll let you rest now," Trey said, his eyes pinning her hostage. "If you need anything at all, just let me know."

There was a whole lot she could think of that she needed from him right now and none of her thoughts required clothes. *Kyra was right. It's been too long since I had sex.* Listening to him talk about his accomplishments affected her in a way she hadn't expected. She was pretty sure her panties were drenched, and all Trey had done was lean against the door.

"Okay," she said, too nervous to voice what she really wanted to ask him for. "I'll let you know if I need anything."

Trey nodded and closed the door behind him. Once she was in the room by herself, she lay back on the bed.

"Why didn't you ask him to stay?" she asked herself quietly. *You know why,* her inner voice taunted. *You're too chicken to tell a man like Trey what you want.* Kiara really didn't understand herself when it came to Trey. Normally, she was never the shy type. She always spoke up when she wanted something. Yet around Trey, all she did was think about everything she wanted to say or do to him without really doing it.

Kiara adjusted herself in the comfortable bed and tried to will herself to go to sleep. Her fear of heights wasn't even an issue at the moment because her arousal was blocking out any other emotion. Thirty minutes later, she was still wide-awake and even worse off than she was before he left.

If you want him, you should go get him. She groaned, annoyed with herself for overthinking the situation. Mind made up, she opened the door and walked down the narrow hallway to the main cabin. The flight attendant saw her first and gave her a wink. *If I didn't know any better, I'd say she knows exactly what I'm up to.*

She approached Trey. *He hasn't turned around yet. Good.* She needed time to figure out what she was going to say.

"Do you need me for something?"

Kiara's eyes flew to the back of Trey's head. "Uh, I was wondering if I could borrow you for a minute." *What the heck? There's nothing sexy about that statement, Kiara!*

"Only a minute, huh?" Trey stood from his seat. "Sure. I'll follow you."

The walk back to the bedroom wasn't nearly long enough to figure out exactly what she would say. Once they were back in the room, Trey closed and locked the door, before leaning his back on it.

"What can I do for you?" he asked. He crossed his arms over his chest the same way he'd done when he was in the bedroom before. His eyes sparked with amusement as he stood there, waiting for her to speak.

"Um. I was wondering. Well, that maybe… If you want to…" Kiara shuffled from one foot to the other before sitting on the bed. *Girl, you aren't making any sense. Get it together!*

"You see. I know what I want. I mean, I think it would help. Actually, I know it would." *Nope, that was just as bad. How about you don't talk anymore?*

She fidgeted with her dress, opting not to say anything else. After a short while, Trey squinted his eyes. "I'm a words person, Kiara. You have to speak up if you want me to know what you're talking about." Trey slyly smiled, which made Kiara want to scream. *He knows damn well what I need.* Now for the question lingering in the air. Was she bold enough to ask for what she wanted?

Taking a deep breath, she went for it. "I'm extremely restless and tense, so I was hoping you could relieve some of my sexual tension." *There, you said it.*

"I'd love to," Trey said with a cocky grin. She'd never seen his cocky grin before, and she had to admit she liked it. "What exactly do you want me to do to relieve your sexual tension?"

"Um, you know…" She let her voice trail off, hoping he got the hint. He didn't.

"I know what?" Trey stepped closer to her and leaned down so that his face was only inches away from hers. "What do you want, sweet Kiara?"

That's it. I'm done with words. Kiara lifted one of his hands into hers and began guiding his hand up her dress and to her thighs. She'd had every intention to remain quiet, but surprisingly, the more aroused she got, the bolder she got.

"I need you to touch me intimately. First, with your hands." She guided his hand even higher. "Then with your breath." She whispered into his ear to convey her meaning. "Lastly, with your tongue." She suckled his bottom lip, moaning at the faint taste of mint and the scotch he'd been sipping on.

"See, now that wasn't so hard," Trey said, before he lifted her by the waist and placed her farther up the bed. Kiara gasped at the movement, clenching the white duvet when Trey's hands began to push her dress above her waist.

"Do you have any idea how long I've been dying to taste you?" Trey said, as he placed soft kisses on her ankles, making his way up her legs.

"No," Kiara said breathlessly. "How long?"

"Ever since I saw you in that white dress and those red pumps at the Rent-a-Bachelor event, I've been dying to dip my tongue into your sweetness."

She felt his fingers slide along the edges of her lacy navy blue panties and drag them down her legs. He hadn't removed her shoes, and truthfully, she didn't want him to do anything that was going to halt her pleasurable journey.

When he kissed her inner thigh, she jerked at the feel of his tongue so close to the part of her that craved him most. "You're soaked," he said. "And now that I know how wet you can get before I even really touch you, it's going to be my main goal to get you this wet all the time."

Kiara began wiggling in the bed. *Lawd, help me.* She was already halfway to an orgasm and he hadn't even kissed her there yet.

"Just breathe." She heard his voice cut through the arousal that was overtaking her mind. He was right. She was barely breathing. Just as she allowed some oxygen into her lungs, she felt his tongue curl around her nub, suckling softly before he dipped his tongue into her center.

Once again, Kiara jerked. Yet this time, Trey held her in place by lacing both his arms under her thighs and dragging her back to the edge of the bed. Kiara dropped her hands and gripped Trey's head instead, keeping him in place. She wasn't sure what she expected to happen when she felt his tongue on her, but his slow languid strokes weren't only stroking her center. He was caressing her mind through his tongue because each stroke made her brain scream with pleasure in the same way her body was craving for a release.

"Trey, please," she begged. At this pace, they'd arrive at their destination before he finished with her, and even though his tongue on her body was sweet torture, she didn't think she could handle it anymore.

Either he didn't hear her, or he refused to listen, because his strokes were still slowly precise, eliciting moans from her that she was sure the staff aboard the flight could hear through the walls.

Suddenly, without warning, Trey increased the pace of his tongue, dipping in and out of her core with a newfound purpose that was driving her to the brink of the edge.

She opened her mouth to ask him what he was doing to her, but no words came out. Only more moans and a noise that she thought may have been a squeal, but she wasn't sure.

Seconds later, her body released a powerful orgasm that rocked her entire being to the core. Her thighs were begging to buck off the bed, but Trey didn't ease his grip. Once she realized he was going to continue to lick her until he got every drop, she gripped his head tighter and held on for the ride. She had no idea how long it took her to come down from her high, but when she did, she noticed Trey had pulled her dress back down over her thighs.

She reached for him with every intention of returning the favor, but Trey lay down beside her and began running his fingers through her hair. Moments later, Kiara didn't see anything but the backs of her eyelids.

Chapter 12

Trey stood back and soaked in the awe-stricken look on Kiara's face as she walked around the luxurious three-story villa overlooking the Ligurian Sea and Monaco, the sovereign city-state located on the French Riviera in Western Europe.

Trey hadn't been to the villa in over three years, but he couldn't imagine it ever looking as beautiful as it did right now.

That's because you're here with her. Kiara makes everything more beautiful.

"This view is breathtaking," she said, walking toward the second-level balcony. The wind blew across her hair and dress the minute she stepped outside.

"You're breathtaking," Trey said. Had he not just tasted her hours prior, he'd be dragging her back inside and into the grand canopy bed that she had yet to see on the third level.

She turned and glanced at him over her shoulder, the sun casting a glow around her face. Unable to help himself, Trey took out his iPhone and snapped a picture before Kiara stepped back inside.

"No fair," she said, walking to him and placing her arms around his waist. "I don't have any pictures of you in my phone."

Trey smiled. "Then I guess you should take plenty before our mini vacation is over. I know I plan to."

Kiara's lips curled to the side in a smile. "I still can't believe your idea of a mini vacation is jet-setting us halfway across the world for an extended weekend. I can't wait to explore this place!"

"Speaking of exploring," Trey said. "A very well-known international film school has a campus here in the French Riviera. A friend of mine asked me if I could speak tonight during a class he teaches. Would you like to accompany me?"

Kiara's eyes lit up. "I'd love to see you in your element. It sounds like fun."

"Great, but I'm warning you… I've been told that I give boring speeches, so don't get your hopes up."

Kiara shook her head. "I can't imagine you being boring at anything." She glanced at the stairwell that led to the third level. "Now, show me the rest of this gorgeous villa so we can head down to the beach before your speech."

Kiara was up the stairs faster than Trey could keep

up. He knew the minute she discovered the grand canopy bed because her gasp echoed through the hallway.

When he reached the top of the stairs and turned the corner, he leaned against the door frame and took a moment to observe her. Her fingers lightly slid across the crisp white sheets and light comforter before her hands moved to the draped white curtains. From there, she observed the vintage dresser and matching nightstand. His housekeeper had left the balcony door slightly ajar as he'd requested earlier this morning, so the curtains around the canopy bed and glass doors that led outside moved lightly with the wind.

"The design of your villa is so unique. I'm not sure what I was expecting, but there is a definite historic vibe to this place. Maybe Victorian age?"

"You have a good eye," Trey said. "This villa was refurbished from the nineteenth century, and when I hired my interior designer, I requested that the villa be kept as authentic as possible. She settled for a mix of Victorian- and Spanish-themed furniture and accent pieces. She even kept the theme consistent when designing my film study."

"Film study?" Kiara asked. "May I see it?"

Although he should have expected the question, it still caught him off guard. Even though his family had been to his villa before, no one besides his designer had ever stepped foot into his film study.

But you want to show her. She's the only one you've ever felt inclined to show. His sister and mom always got on his case about being so private about showing certain parts of his home, but for some reason, he didn't want to be private around Kiara. If she was interested, he wanted to show her everything. "Sure," he said, taking her hand in his. "Come with me."

She smiled in a way that was slowly becoming his most favorite vision in the world. He led her to the end of the hallway where a small table and lamp sat in the corner. Right above the table was his favorite *Encyclopedia Britannica* collection, placed on three built-in shelves.

"Wow," Kiara said. "I haven't seen an entire encyclopedia collection in years."

"My grandfather passed it down to my mom and she passed the collection down to me," Trey said.

"I'm surprised you keep it in the villa and not back at your home in LA."

Trey smiled before pulling out one of the encyclopedias and handing it to Kiara. She flipped through a few pages before glancing up at him. "It's not the original, is it? It looks the same, but knowing you, there's no way you wouldn't have this collection in your sight."

Trey laughed. "You guessed right. This is an exact replica of the encyclopedias that I keep back in LA. Remind me to show you where they are next time you're at my home."

Kiara placed the book back on the shelf and glanced around the small corner. "I assume this corner isn't your film study. Or is it?"

"It's not." Trey reached for the seventh encyclopedia on the shelf and bent it forward. As the wall turned to the side to reveal a narrow hallway, his eyes stayed pinned to Kiara, soaking in her surprised expression.

"Trey Moore, you never cease to surprise me."

"After you," Trey said as he motioned for Kiara to walk down the hallway. He thought she might hesitate given that the lighting was dim, but she walked right through the opening and stopped when she reached the entrance of his film study.

"This is…" Kiara's voice trailed off when she stepped into the room. Trey knew his study like the back of his hand, but watching her run her fingers along the framed posters of the movies he'd written screenplays for forced him to view the room through a different set of eyes.

"This room used to serve as a safe house," he explained. "I had the skylights in the ceiling added, but other than that, it's authentic to the original design." The study was divided into three different sections, with his grand mahogany desk in the main section. The skylights provided ample natural light for the space, and built-in bookshelves housed his private library.

"All the books on the top level are based on some of my favorite Hollywood and independent films," Trey said when Kiara made her way to the bookshelves. "I also have books about the film industry, writing quirks and other information that's aided me in my journey."

Kiara walked into the next room that contained replicas of all the plaques and awards he'd won in the industry. The room also had a large beige chaise lounge, a small bar and a refrigerator.

"The door in the corner leads to a modest bathroom," Trey said. "That way, I never have to leave when I'm in the moment or on a deadline."

"Forget the villa," Kiara said. "I could live in your film study alone."

Trey laughed. "That's the idea. I've always felt that way, but I've never shown this room to anyone besides my designer. I'm glad you share the feeling, too."

Kiara squinted. "You've never shown anyone your study before?"

Trey shook his head. Kiara observed him for a few more seconds before she pointed to a built-in safe he'd forgotten was in the room as well. "I like the safe. I almost didn't notice the dial."

"How do you know it isn't fake?"

She lifted an eyebrow. "Is it?"

Trey glanced at the wall. "No, it's real. It was designed to mesh with the filmography design on the accent wall. It holds all my important electronics while I'm away. Mainly, backup laptops and hard drives."

Kiara nodded as she walked into the third room. He sensed something more was on her mind, but she remained quiet.

Trey watched her stand in the middle of the empty room and glance up at the ceiling. "It's been years, but I'm still not sure what to do with this room," he said. "Every time I think I have an idea, I overanalyze it. By the time I'm done second-guessing, the idea doesn't seem to fit anymore."

Kiara glanced around the room before looking back at him. "You write screenplays and you're obviously a movie buff. Why not design this room as an old-school movie theater complete with a vintage popcorn machine?" She waved her hands around the center of the room. "In this space, you could have recliner chairs or even a large sectional with enough room for you to stretch out. And since I notice you love accent walls, the accent wall in this room could be the names of all the film directors, writers and producers that you admire written creatively on the wall."

Trey stepped farther into the empty room, suddenly very aware as to why his ideas had never worked in the past. "That sounds perfect," he said, stepping closer to her. He glanced around the empty space and could visualize everything Kiara had stated.

"I'll call the designer tomorrow morning."

Kiara laughed. "Just like that?"

"Just like that." He brushed her cheek with the back of his hand. "There's only one thing that could make it better."

Her eyes bounced across his face. "What's that?"

"If every time you accompany me on a trip to my villa, we watch a movie together in this room."

Her lips slightly parted in surprise. Trey knew what he was doing. Without saying the words, he was letting her know that he wanted to make plans for the future with her. Not only did he value her opinion, but he wanted her in his life more permanently.

"Why am I the only person you've ever welcomed into your film study?"

Trey studied her eyes. "You're the only person I've ever wanted to share my film study with."

"Not even your mom and sister have seen this space?"

"Nope. Not even my mom and sister. They tease me on being so private about opening up certain parts of my home with others, but I can't help it. I've always felt like there should be at least one room in your home that is sacredly yours."

Kiara nodded. "I understand that. Yet you decided to share this with me? And you mentioned other visits."

Trey looped his arms around her waist and pulled her even closer to him. "I'm beginning to realize that there isn't a part of me or my home that I don't want to share with you. And yes, I hope there will be plenty more visits to this villa in our future. That is, if you see me in your future as well."

Kiara smiled as she entwined her arms around Trey's neck. "As much as I've tried to fight it, a future with you is all I've been imagining lately. Although I must admit, it scares the hell out of me."

"Me, too," Trey said with a laugh. "I've never felt this way about anyone before, but I welcome these feelings that we haven't even defined yet."

"Haven't defined or just haven't admitted out loud?"

Trey's eyes briefly dropped to her lips. "I guess a little bit of both. What do you think?"

"I'd agree with that assessment." Kiara leaned her head on his chest. "Are we completely insane to be feeling so strongly about one another when we still have so much more to learn about each other?"

"We could be," he said, placing his chin on the top of her head. "But I'm willing to see where this path leads us if you are."

"I'm in," she said, lifting her head. He was sure she'd parted her lips to say something else, but Trey stole a kiss before any more words could be spoken. He didn't understand how it was possible, but each time he kissed Kiara, it felt stronger than the time before. Before they went back to the States, he'd lay out all his feelings and pray that he didn't scare her away. If he sensed hesitation on her part, he'd try to scale back his feelings.

Kiara deepened the kiss, eliciting a groan from Trey. *Screw it. With lips like hers, scaling back is the last thing on my mind.*

"Pardon me," Kiara said as she made her way to the seat that had been reserved for her. The auditorium was packed with well over three hundred students, and Kiara was excited for Trey's speech.

After Kiara had suggested a way to design Trey's empty room in his film study, they'd spent the rest of the day talking about designs and walking around the neighborhood. They hadn't made it to the beach, and before they knew it, it was almost time for Trey's speech. They'd only had enough time to shower and change.

After a little bit of rushing, they'd arrived with ten minutes to spare, which only allowed enough time for a brief introduction to Trey's friend, Professor Louis Arthur, and his assistant, who showed Kiara to her seat toward the front of the auditorium.

Small conversation was taking place all around her, and although French was the most prominent language being spoken, she heard quite a bit of English. She smiled at a couple of students seated next to her.

"Are you visiting?" a female student asked in a heavy French accent.

"Yes," Kiara said. "I just arrived today. My friend is a guest speaker for tonight's class."

"Guest speaker," a young man said. "Is your friend Trey Moore, the world-renowned screenwriter?"

Kiara nodded. "Yes, that's correct. Have you heard of him?"

"Heard of him?" the female student said. "We idolize him here. His last screenplay was nominated for awards that most of us dream of winning one day."

The man nodded in agreement. "He's very well-known in our town. And his donations to the film program at the university have given a lot of us opportunities and internships that we wouldn't have otherwise."

Kiara was curious to chat more with the students, but the lights dimmed, signaling the start of the class. She sat a little straighter in her seat as Trey and Professor Arthur walked onto the stage.

Professor Arthur began speaking in French, and Kiara was grateful for the English subtitles on the back screen that she could follow along. When the professor announced Trey, the audience erupted in applause. Kiara clapped and whistled along with everyone else, a huge smile on her face when he winked at her.

"Thank you so much, ladies and gentlemen," Trey said. "I appreciate the warm welcome."

Kiara's eyes bounced from Trey to the words on the screen written in French, interpreting what he was saying to the audience.

Trey cleared his throat. "My French is a little rusty, but I'll do my best to speak as fluently as possible." When Trey opened his mouth and spoke his first French words of the night, Kiara was sure she'd melted in her seat. *He sounds beautiful.* She had never been a fan of men with accents. It wasn't that she didn't like them; she was just indifferent. Her sister used to tease her about being the only woman on the planet who didn't find accents sexy, and that was okay with her.

Okay, sis, Kiara thought. *I get it now.* Never had a man sounded as sexy as a French-speaking Trey. *Except for maybe the English-speaking Trey.* And even then, Trey with an accent was giving Trey without an accent a run for his money.

As Trey dived into his speech, Kiara didn't even mind the fact that she had to read the screen to understand what he was saying. The entire room was captivated as he went through the top ten rules every writer should follow when writing a screenplay.

His voice wasn't the only thing she found hypnotizing. Trey walked around the stage in a way that commanded everyone's attention. It wasn't just his stylish light gray suit or freshly cut hair that made him appealing to the eye. It was the way he stood still when his voice dropped to a serious tone. It was the way he positioned his hands when emphasizing an important point. It was the way his lips curled to the side in a sneaky smile when he was making a joke about something. Every single move he made had Kiara's undivided attention, and soon, the room faded away and all she saw was Trey passionately speaking about his favorite topic.

When he neared the end of his speech and asked if there were any questions, hands rose across the room before he'd even finished speaking. He promised to answer at least fifteen of the forty people who had questions for him.

After he took a few questions, he pointed to the female student who was sitting next to Kiara.

"Thanks for speaking to our class today, Mr. Moore," she said in English. "Most of us have followed your career for years, and it seems that every year, you write more and more screenplays. I wanted to know—on average, how many screenplays do you write in a year and how do you stay motivated in your writing?"

"That's a good question," Trey said. "On average, I write about eight screenplays a year, but next year, I suspect that number will increase to eleven."

At the gasps in the audience, Trey smiled. *If I could bottle up that smile, I would.*

"However, I'll be the first to admit that, lately, writing for me hasn't held the same joy that it once had." Trey took a sip of water before continuing. "I used to live and breathe my words, but a few years ago, I began to lose my way. I was at the peak of my career and had just won two prestigious awards, yet I felt lost in my craft.

"As a writer, there will be times when you are so engrossed in a project that you can see the success even before you've completed the work. Then there are other times when no matter how dedicated you are to your work, you lose focus and the words don't seem to flow as well. I believe that the important thing to realize during those times is that every screenplay you write doesn't have to be a Hollywood hit. Sometimes, a screenplay may pull you in different directions, and the purpose of writing the screenplay may not be to create the next big hit, but rather, discover a part of yourself that you may have never tapped into before. When I write, I try to put a piece of my heart into my work in hopes that in doing so, I will better relate to the screenplay I'm working on."

The audience remained quiet, immersed in Trey's confession. "When you encounter an issue in the story that keeps you from moving forward, the key is to look for solutions to help your plot. Most of the time, those solutions are in the small details of the story. Details that may help you move along a scene and are necessary to the story." Trey's lips curled to the side in a smile. "Other times, the solution to help your plot may not be in the story at all, but rather, the inspiration you need to fulfill your duty as a screenplay writer. It may be in a hobby you enjoy or a new experience. Maybe even a creative writing prompt to get you out of your current mind-set." Trey's eyes found hers. "Or the solution may be in a person who manages to steal a piece of your heart and force you to feel things you never have before and view life through a different set of eyes."

Trey broke eye contact with her and pointed to the audience. "You see, the key to figuring out what you need to reach your fullest potential is to first figure out what your goal is as a screenwriter. What is your purpose? Whose story are you telling? Every person in this room has a story, and when you're a screenwriter, you're not only the star of the story in some way, shape or form, but the narrator of the story as well. Don't be afraid to create your own personal style of writing and make sure you check your ego at the door. As writers, you have to be willing to let your words speak for themselves, so when I say check your ego, I'm talking about stepping out of your own way. No one can label you as a failure. Only you can do that. You hold all the power to your destiny. Never forget that."

Trey answered a few more questions, but Kiara couldn't even focus on the responses anymore. She was too busy trying to get her heart to stop beating so fast. Not only had he impressed her, but she'd been able to relate to his speech even though she wasn't the target audience. It had been a long time since she'd heard a speech that touched her to her core. Given that the speaker was Trey was just icing on a seven-layer cake.

Chapter 13

Trey glanced over at Kiara, who was looking out of the car window into the night sky. "Is everything okay? You've been quiet since we left the university."

"I'm fine," she said, turning to him. "Just soaking in the beautiful view." They were driving down the main road that overlooked the beautiful Ligurian Sea. His villa was only a few blocks away.

Trey tapped the driver of his car. "If you could let us off right here at this corner, we'll walk the rest of the way."

"Are you sure? There is a storm coming," the driver said.

"We're sure." Trey looked at Kiara to see if she would hesitate, but she didn't. Once they were out of the vehicle, he grabbed Kiara's hand and began walking toward the villa. "Okay, now that we're in the fresh night air, do you care to tell me why you're so quiet tonight?"

Kiara glanced up at Trey and smiled. "You were amazing tonight and were far from boring like you claimed to be."

Trey shrugged. "I have my moments."

"No, I'm pretty sure your speeches are always that enlightening. I wasn't purposely being quiet tonight, but I guess your speech made me reflect on my own life and my own path."

Trey glanced around and decided to take a shortcut through the beach. Once their feet touched the smooth sand, he felt Kiara release some of her tension. "I'm glad that you enjoyed my speech, but you've accomplished a lot in your career. In case you didn't know, you run the most elite and successful preschool and day care in LA."

"Thank you," Kiara said. "You're right—I've had a lot of success in my career, but in some other areas, I could use a few improvements."

"Areas like what?"

Kiara bit her bottom lip. "Areas like relationships. I've had the worst luck and I'm wondering if…" Her voice trailed off as they approached the ocean.

"Wondering if what?" Trey asked, turning her to face him. He sensed whatever she didn't want to say had to do with him. "In case you need me to be clearer," Trey said, "I want to be in an exclusive relationship with you. I want to see where this goes."

"I want that, too," Kiara said in a soft voice. "But I wonder if you'd still want to be in a relationship with me if you knew the truth."

Trey studied her eyes. "The truth about what? There isn't anything you could say that would make me not interested."

The eyes staring back at him still looked unsure. When she turned to stare out into the ocean, he followed suit. They stood there for a few moments, neither saying anything as it began to drizzle outside.

"Kiara," he said. "I don't know what it is that you're afraid to tell me, but I can tell you that what I'm feeling won't fade. I'm falling for you, Kiara Woods. And I'm falling pretty damn hard."

She turned to him, her lips parting as she searched his eyes. Raindrops fell across her face, but she didn't seem to mind. "I'm falling for you, too," she said. "And it happened so fast I didn't even know what I was feeling until you were already in my heart."

Trey lowered his head at the same time that Kiara stood on her tiptoes. He expected their kiss to be frenzied given the desire they felt for one another, but the kiss was slow and seductive. Kiara met the strokes of his tongue with bold strokes of her own, each coaxing feelings from the other that were impossible to deny.

The loud crackle of thunder caused them to break off. "We should head back to the villa," Trey said. Kiara nodded, and together, they grasped hands and made a run in the direction of the villa. Within seconds, the soft drizzle turned into huge raindrops.

"This is crazy," Kiara yelled through the falling rain.

Trey glanced around the beach and spotted an enclosed lifeguard stand. "Come on. We can wait out some of the storm in there."

They ran, still hand in hand, in the direction of the lifeguard stand that was a few feet away. Trey could have sworn that there was usually a ramp to walk up to the stand, but it had been years since he'd been on this beach. All he saw now was a wooden ladder to climb up.

"You first," he said to Kiara as he helped her to the ladder. Once they were both inside, Trey was relieved to find two battery-operated lanterns and several beach towels stacked in the corner. He wasted no time laying out the towels and turning on the lanterns.

"Wow," Kiara said as she looked outside the small front window of the stand. "I've never seen anything like that."

Trey walked over to stand beside her and observe the storm. Although the lightning wasn't close to them, the way it lit up the ocean and increased the size of the waves made it appear much closer than it was.

"Apparently, being away for so long made me forget how quickly the storms start out here."

"Apparently," Kiara said with a laugh. She lifted her hand to the top of her head and ran her fingers through her hair. "I usually love the rain, but I'm sure my hair makes me look like a wet dog right now, which is not cute. Be prepared for it to go full-blown poodle in a few minutes."

Trey joined in her laughter. "You're still just as beautiful." He pulled her closer to him, and when she began lifting her legs, he caught her thighs in his hand, neither breaking their kiss. When he pinned her between him and the wall of the lifeguard stand, their kiss grew even deeper. He moved from her lips down to her neck, kissing the swells of her breasts peeking through the top of the sleek black dress she'd chosen to wear for his speech.

"It sounds pretty bad out there," Kiara said breathlessly.

"Which is precisely why we're staying here until the storm lets up," he said as his lips made their way back up her neck. Her sweet moans mingled with the sound of the rain pounding against the lifeguard stand. When Kiara stepped out of his embrace, it took all his energy not to pull her back. She pointed for him to lean against the wall, and Trey did as he was told.

"I think we should take advantage of this storm," she said quietly. Her hands made their way to her dress, as she slowly eased each strap from her shoulders. Within seconds, the dress fell in a puddle around her feet, revealing her black lace pantie and bra set. Next, she eased his suit jacket off his shoulders and began unbuttoning his dress shirt. Trey felt like he was holding his breath in anticipation of what she would do next.

"There's a chance someone else is stuck in this storm and will come here," he said. He didn't want to jeopardize the moment, but he wanted Kiara to be well aware of the fact that they were in a public place.

"I'm game if you are," she said with a sly smile as she ran her hands down his chest and over his abs before unbuckling his pants.

"I'm definitely game." Trey helped her slide his pants and boxers off and kicked them to the side to join the rest of their clothes. He'd never been shy about his nudity and the hungry look in Kiara's eyes was one he'd been waiting to see since they'd met. He almost laughed at the amount of times her eyes dropped down to his erection, but he didn't want to ruin the moment. So instead, he let her stand there and look her fill.

"You're beautiful," she said as she ran her fingers over his arms and down the sides of his thighs.

"Men aren't beautiful. Women are."

Kiara shook her head. "I beg to differ because you, Trey Moore, are the most beautiful man I've ever seen. Inside and out."

Trey slightly closed his eyes and relished her words. He'd been called beautiful before by other women, but never had the words affected him like they did when Kiara said them. With Kiara, he knew she truly saw his heart and she wasn't just basing her statement on looks.

He reached for her, but once again Kiara stepped back from him. Only this time, she moved closer to one of the lanterns. "I want you to see me," she said as she began sliding a bra strap over her shoulder. He noticed her hands slightly shook as she continued to undress and Trey wasn't sure if it was nerves, or the chill from getting caught in the rain.

She tossed her bra to the side and turned around so that her back was facing him. "All of me," she said as her fingers looped around the edge of her panties and she dragged them down over her hips and tossed them to the side as well. Her backside was just as plump as he'd imagined and Trey wasn't sure if he'd ever seen anything sexier than the way Kiara looked right now.

"Men from my past haven't really seen me," she said, turning around to face him. When she did, his breath caught in his throat. He already knew she was beautiful and downright sexy in clothes. However, completely nude, Kiara was breathtaking. He was completely mesmerized by her. *You were mesmerized even before today*, his inner voice reminded him.

With every day that he spent with Kiara, she was becoming more and more of a permanent fixture in his life. She was someone he couldn't wait to see and someone he missed terribly when she wasn't around. Yet that wasn't the only reason he was captivated by Kiara. He knew that there was still more to learn about each other and he wanted to know everything about her. Her secrets. What made her tick. What made her smile. He noticed a couple of scars on her perfect body and wanted to know how she'd gotten them. He was anxious to discover every level of her desire.

Trey walked over to Kiara and lightly lifted her chin. Even now, the eyes staring back at him held secrets that she didn't dare tell him until she was ready. And he didn't only see unspoken secrets in her depths. He saw pain and hurt. He saw that she'd put herself out there one too many times only to be rejected by someone she'd thought had loved her. He saw a woman who usually guarded her heart, yet here she was, opening herself up to him in ways that he assumed she'd never thought she would.

Trey leaned a little closer and tilted her chin a little higher. "I see you," he said, his voice barely above a whisper. "I see your strength. Your passion. Your determination. Your ability to overcome the obstacles life has thrown your way. Kiara Woods, I see you and all I want is to continue seeing everything you're willing to share with me."

The smile that filled her face right before she gripped the back of his neck and pulled him in for a kiss was one that Trey considered his favorite smile of hers. It was the perfect mix of sexy and sweet…just like her.

Carefully, Trey eased them both down to the bed of towels he'd laid out when they first arrived. He continued to kiss her as she lifted her legs around his waist and met the strokes of his tongue. Reaching for his pants, he quickly got out the condom in his wallet and sheathed himself. Her hands gripped his arms as she resumed kissing him breathless, moving to his neck and collarbone.

"Are you sure?" he whispered, looking down into her eyes.

"Very," she said as she reached down in between their bodies and guided him into her entrance. She moaned when he was partially inside her and Trey didn't need any additional confirmation.

Slowly. Precisely. He began moving his hips to a rhythm he would always refer to as the K&T rhythm because he'd only been inside her for seconds and already he was feeling things that he'd never felt before.

Trey slightly lifted her hips to get a better fit and was rewarded when he slid even deeper into Kiara. She was so tight that he was worried he might hurt her if he tilted her hips any more. But Kiara didn't seem to mind. She lifted her hips the rest of the way, and once he was fully embedded in her, they both stopped moving and savored the moment.

"You're perfect," he whispered to Kiara as he began moving again. She smiled and met his thrusts, her moans mixing with the beat of the raindrops pounding on the roof of the lifeguard stand. It didn't matter that they were on the floor. It didn't matter that the beach was probably slightly flooded from the storm. It didn't even matter that Trey knew the beach patrol would be checking all the lifeguard stands soon to see if anyone was taking shelter there to avoid the storm. All that mattered to him was the seductive dance that he and Kiara were currently doing. She was his only focus and bringing her the utmost pleasure was his only goal.

Lifting Kiara to adjust her body underneath him, he angled her legs in a way that he knew would give him the best chance of hitting her G-spot. Her soft cry echoed across the space as he measured his strokes while teasing her plump brown nipples at the same time.

"Trey," she said breathlessly. "I think… I'm about…"

Although she couldn't get the words out, Trey knew the signs. She was teetering on the edge of an orgasm and he was right there with her.

"Me, too," he whispered into her ear. "Come for me, baby. Let me hear that soft orgasm cry." Almost on cue, Kiara released her orgasm, her hips bucking forcefully and her core squeezing his shaft in a way that caused Trey's eyes to roll to the back of his head.

"Damn," he groaned as he followed suit minutes after Kiara. He tried to stop the convulsions so that he could focus on eliciting more pleasure for her, but his climax was so powerful that it sucked up all his energy. Trey rolled over to his side, careful not to crush her, and pulled Kiara along with him so that she was now on top of him.

"Wow," Kiara said after a few minutes.

"Wow is right."

She stretched on top of him and groaned. "Ouch. It hurts to move."

"Sorry," Trey said, brushing some of her wet hair out of her face. "Maybe next time we'll have time for foreplay."

"We've had weeks of foreplay," Kiara said with a smile. "We needed this night exactly how it was."

Trey looked down at Kiara. "You mean in a lifeguard stand, in the middle of a storm, with only a couple lanterns and a handful of beach towels to keep us from getting splinters? You're right. We needed exactly this."

Kiara laughed. "No, smart-ass. That's not what I meant."

"I know what you meant." Trey pulled her a little closer. "And I think tonight was perfect. I wouldn't change anything about it."

A knock on the door caused them both to jump. "Sir, ma'am," the voice said. "This stand is supposed to be locked, so I'm going to ask you to gather your things and leave."

"Oh my God," Kiara whispered. "Who is that?"

"I assume it's beach patrol. Come on." Trey helped Kiara to her feet and was careful to keep her blocked from the cutout window.

"There's no glass in that window," she said as she began getting dressed. "Do you think he heard us having sex?"

"I did, ma'am," the voice answered on the other side of the door. "We get this sort of thing all the time. I didn't want to interrupt."

Kiara looked at Trey and her eyes widened. "I don't know if we should be grateful or embarrassed."

"Grateful," Trey said, giving her a quick kiss on the lips. Once they were dressed, Trey hastily folded back the towels and turned off the lanterns. They opened the door, and as expected, a young man from beach patrol was waiting on the platform. To Trey, he didn't look to be any older than twenty-five.

"Sorry about that," Trey said. The rainfall was back to the drizzle that it was before they went seeking shelter.

The young man shrugged. "Don't mention it. I came by earlier, but I didn't want to interrupt." Trey laughed, but Kiara looked horrified.

After they'd climbed down the ladder, Kiara turned to face Trey. "Do you think we should tell him that those towels need to be washed?"

"I'm sure he already knows," Trey said. "But you can tell him if it will make you feel better."

Kiara crossed her arms over her chest. "You don't think I have the guts to tell him?"

He quirked an eyebrow at her. "You looked mortified every time the guy said anything to us."

"Watch this." Kiara walked back to the lifeguard stand and climbed the ladder. Trey was still waiting in the same spot when she returned.

"Well, did you tell him?" he asked when Kiara walked

past him toward the direction of the villa and didn't say anything.

"I didn't need to," she said with a shrug.

"Why not?"

Kiara looked back at the lifeguard stand and waved at the beach patrol guy, who was laughing at them as they walked away. "I didn't need to because he'd already packed the towels in a plastic bag."

Trey nodded and noticed she had something in her hand. "Is that all that happened?"

"Um." Kiara glanced down at the small plastic bag in her hand. "He told me to have a good night and handed me this." She thrust the plastic bag into Trey's hand. Trey opened the bag and pulled out a small piece of clothing.

"Are these your—"

"Are those my panties? Yes, Trey, they are. And if you so much as say a peep about this ever again, we will never have sex again."

Trey tried to hold in his laugh, but he couldn't. "You're so adorable when you're embarrassed," Trey said, pinching her cheeks before backing away from her.

"I warned you," she said as she took off after him. They ran the rest of the way to the villa, neither too anxious to end all the fun they were having outside in the rain.

Chapter 14

"Trey, I thought you promised me a romantic day trip with beautiful scenery and breathtaking views?"

"I did," Trey said from in front of her. "Isn't this view spectacular?"

Kiara glanced over the side of the cliff they were currently hiking up and immediately retreated. "I'm not sure *spectacular* is the right word. More like terrifying."

"Oh, come on." Trey walked back to where Kiara was gripping a small tree on the side of the cliff. "I thought you said you enjoyed hiking?"

Kiara gave him the side-eye. "Enjoyed? I'm pretty sure I said that my siblings and I once hiked through the woods at Lake Tahoe when our mom took us on vacation there once, and it was better than I thought it would be."

"Exactly," Trey said. "Maybe I embellished what you said a little, but in my defense, I'd already planned on taking you here before our conversation this morning."

Kiara placed her hand in Trey's outstretched one as he helped her up. "Can't we just go back to the villa and continue the fun we started last night?" Kiara batted her eyes and gave her best sweet girl smile.

Last night in the lifeguard stand she'd had some of the best sex of her life. After they'd been asked to leave by beach patrol, they'd opted not to return to the villa right away and spent the rest of the night walking in the light rain and talking about their pasts and certain circumstances that had led them to where they were today.

Once they'd gotten back to the villa, they'd continued the fun by having sex in the shower, and Kiara had been speechless when Trey had offered to wash her hair. The entire night had been magical, and she hadn't wanted it to end.

When Trey had awakened her with a good-morning kiss and told her breakfast was ready, her fantasy vacation continued as they talked over coffee and eggs. She'd just known that the rest of the day would be equally as memorable—only they'd been hiking for an hour already, and she was ready to pass out.

Kiara groaned as she followed Trey around a narrow corner. *Worst day to wear shorts.* Her blue jean shorts were riding up her thighs and her white T-shirt was slightly dirty from all the times she'd wiped the sweat from her brow. She groaned even louder when she noticed Trey's gray basketball shorts and white T still looked flawless. Not a smidgen of dirt.

"You do realize that last night I worked muscles that I haven't worked in a while, right?"

Trey laughed. "Meaning?"

She waited to respond until they reached a wider opening. "Meaning my thighs are burning, my calves are sore and my neck has a knot in it that I can't work out."

"I'm sorry, baby," Trey said as he reached back to hold her hand now that they could walk side by side. "But I promise you'll love where we're going. Only ten more minutes and we'll be there."

Kiara yelped in pain when her gym shoe hit a large rock. "I'm not convinced."

"Then let's talk about something else to take your mind off it," Trey suggested. "Do you want to hear something strange?"

"Sure."

Trey sighed. "Although I'm having a fantastic time with you on this mini vacation, I also find myself missing M-dog."

"Aww," Kiara said. "That's so cute. Why would you call that strange?"

"I don't know," Trey said with a shrug. "I guess it's because I never really thought the kid would hold such a special place in my heart when he's not even old enough to talk yet."

Kiara smiled. "I'm not surprised. You're really great with him and it's obvious that he loves you a lot, too. Some may think that babies are too young to have a good sense of character, but I disagree. It's true that some babies are colicky, and they may cry regardless of the person with them. But I think it's also true that other babies pick up on a person's true character traits. If you're not a good person, a baby or an infant will notice. I've often told parents who sign up for counseling at LA Little Ones that they need to listen to what their baby is trying to tell them."

"I didn't know you offered counseling," Trey said. "Is there anything you don't do?"

"Well," Kiara said with a sneaky smile. "Up until last month, I didn't date a parent or guardian of any of my little ones. But a very pushy uncle insisted that I go to his home and help him take care of his nephew. Then he wined me and dined me. He even had the audacity to take me on a vacation halfway around the world."

Trey laughed. "Oh, no, you don't. If my memory serves me right, you hired me for a day to show me how to care for my nephew, and although I appreciate your help, that was all your idea. And I'm not M-dog's parent or guardian, so you didn't break any personal rules for me."

"Temporary guardian counts," Kiara said. "Besides, we've gotten off topic. Getting back to what you said, I think it's great that you miss Matthew. It shows how much you care."

"You only changed the topic because you know I'm right," Trey said. "But since I love talking about M-dog, I'll let it slide. I guess what I was getting at is that being around M-dog has really made me feel things I never thought I would."

Kiara kept her head faced on the path ahead of her

as her heartbeat quickened. She had a feeling she knew exactly where this conversation was headed.

"What does being around him make you feel?" she asked, despite herself.

Trey sighed. "I already told you how bad it was growing up without Reginald, and even though my stepfather was around, we never really got that close father-son bond. He's a good man and a good father to my sister, Carmen, but I learned early on that I didn't have the makings of a great father. At least I thought I didn't. Since I was never the player type, I think most of my family and close friends figured I would eventually settle down and start a family of my own. But I never wanted that. I never even thought I could have that."

Kiara glanced over at Trey, who seemed lost in thought. *Now is the time, Kiara. Now is the time to remind him.* "Trey," she said. "Do you remember when we were having dinner a while back and I told you that I don't want kids?"

"Yes, I remember."

She stopped walking and turned to face him. "Well, I still feel that way. I don't want kids and that's not something that will change as we get closer. I've dated men in the past who thought they could change me, and they were sadly mistaken."

Trey squinted his eyes. "I can't say I understand why, because you'd make a terrific mother," he said. "But I respect your decision and I won't try to change that."

He says that now, but he can't mean it. "I've heard that before, too."

Trey lightly touched her cheek. "Who was he? Who

was the guy that made it difficult for you to believe what I'm saying? Was it your ex-husband?"

Kiara glanced away and stared out into the mountains. "Yes, it was. My ex-husband and I split because of it. After that, my last boyfriend decided on the day that he was going to propose that he couldn't handle my decision." She glanced back at Trey as her mind went back to the moment she'd told her ex-husband and ex-boyfriend about her inability to have children. "Men always say that they are fine with continuing a relationship that doesn't involve kids, until they actually consider what it means. I know what you were getting at earlier. Being around M-dog is showing you a different side of yourself. The side that sees he will make a great father one day despite the fact that he thought fatherhood wasn't in his future."

"It isn't."

"It is," Kiara said. "Trey, it's so clear that you want to be a father."

"Kiara, I want you and only you. I didn't bring up M-dog to make you upset. I was just saying how I didn't know my heart could love a little person so fast. That's all I meant by it."

Kiara studied his eyes and saw in them a man who may say he never wanted to be a father, but deep down, probably craved fatherhood most of all. *You'll have to give him up eventually, Kiara. He'll start to want things you can't give him.*

Kiara turned and began hiking the way they were originally going. Even if Trey didn't want to acknowledge what was so clearly written in his eyes, she could decipher his feelings on her own. *But giving him up doesn't mean it has to be today.* She couldn't even end their relationship now if she wanted to. She was too far from home and way too invested in Trey for it to end based on her hypothetical assumption.

Her thoughts ceased the minute she reached the top of the cliff that opened into level ground and revealed the most beautiful trees and turquoise water she'd ever seen.

"This is magnificent," she whispered when she felt Trey stand beside her.

"It's my favorite part of the Southern Alps," Trey said, placing his arm around her shoulders. "I've gotten some good writing done in this place. Plus, I swear the air smells fresher up here."

Kiara closed her eyes and took a deep breath. "I think you're right. The air definitely smells better."

Trey kissed the side of her neck while her eyes were still closed. The way he kissed her made her feel like they hadn't just had a disagreement. And the fact that he could move on from it, instead of making it a bigger issue, touched her heart.

Just another reason I'm falling in love with this man. Her eyes flew open at her thought. She'd already admitted she was falling for him, so typically, that meant falling in love, not that she just liked him. However, the fact that she'd thought the word *love* so effortlessly meant she'd say it just as easily in front of Trey. Hell, she'd already spoken some thoughts aloud in front of him before.

Trey wrinkled his forehead in concern. "Are you okay?"

"Um, yes. I'm fine. This place is just breathtaking."

"Almost as breathtaking as my current company." His eyes dropped to her lips. "I made us get out so early because it's always pretty empty around this time. Come on. Let's go for a swim in the natural pool before anyone else arrives."

Kiara tossed her mini backpack next to Trey's. She hesitated when her hands went to her blue jean shorts. "I didn't wear a bathing suit," Kiara said.

"Who says you need one," he said as he removed his shirt and basketball shorts, leaving him in only his blue boxers. Boxers that did nothing to tame Kiara's naughty thoughts.

Trey was jumping off the ramp and into the water before she'd even removed her shorts. Once she'd removed her clothes, she walked over to the edge of the ramp. She was amazed at how see-through the water was and immediately noticed the rock, coral and fish in their natural habitat.

"Uh, how deep is it?" She'd snorkeled before and enjoyed it. However, the fact that she could see everything was making her a little nervous. She glanced up when Trey hadn't responded to her question.

"What's wrong?" she asked, unable to read the look on his face.

"That's what you choose to wear underneath your hiking clothes?"

She glanced down at her peach panties that were cut out on the sides with three strings attaching both sides and the matching crop-top bralette. "If you remember correctly, you never told me we'd be doing this much hiking. Had I known, I would have worn something more appropriate."

"I'm glad you didn't," Trey said, treading the water. "That's the sexiest lingerie I've ever seen. I'm worried even the fish will want you, as good as you look in it."

Kiara laughed at Trey's corniness. With Trey, she was doing things she'd never done before. Having experiences she'd never had before. Facing fears she would have sworn she'd never face. With Trey, she was learning more about herself than she had with all her exes combined.

Getting over her nerves, Kiara took a step back, then ran and jumped into the water close to where Trey was. She surfaced quickly, but Trey was right there beside her, brushing her hair out of her eyes and asking her if she was okay.

"I'm okay," she said with a big smile. "What do we do next?"

Trey laughed. "You just got in, and already you're up for another adventure." Kiara nodded.

"Okay," Trey said. "Follow me."

They swam to the corner of the natural pool, and Kiara could tell by the distance of the coral underneath that it had gotten deeper.

"You okay?" Trey asked as he pulled back some long vines that were hanging into the water.

"I think so," she said. "I'm just trying not to think about how deep it is or how much bigger the fish are over here."

"They won't bite," he said, taking her hand. "It's going to be dark for a couple seconds. Then it will lighten up. If you get nervous, just grip my hand harder."

When it darkened, Kiara was too nervous to even open her eyes. She just stayed close by Trey and ignored anything she felt graze against her leg in the water. Within seconds, she felt the floor of the natural pool signaling they could stand up.

"We're here," Trey said, leading them out the water and onto a smooth black surface.

"Is this a cave?" Kiara asked as she glanced around at the rocks and holes in the top that allowed for sunlight to shine through.

"Yes, it's natural black rock and it's been like this for decades. A couple locals showed me this place years ago, and any chance I get, I come up here." Trey motioned for them to sit on the rock.

"I've never seen anything like this," Kiara said. "The blackness of the rock makes it appear harsh, but it's the smoothest rock I've ever felt."

Trey nodded. "The combination of the coral and water almost acts as sandpaper, carving down the rock until it's smooth, and people like us are able to lie out here and enjoy one of the beauties of nature."

Kiara scooted closer to Trey, glad that they were the only people around. "Have you ever brought anyone else here?"

Trey shook his head. "Never. You're the first and only person I've ever wanted to bring here."

Kiara ran her fingers down his chest. "And we're pretty secluded in here, right?"

"I think so," he said. "Usually when I'm here by my-self, I can hear when other people arrive at the natural pool. I can't hear anyone out there yet."

"Good," Kiara said as she motioned for him to lie on his back.

"What are you doing?" he asked, his voice huskier than it had been moments before.

Kiara curled her lips to the side in a smile. "What do you think?" She positioned herself in between his legs and got on her knees. "I've been waiting to taste you for a long time, Mr. Moore." Kiara pulled down his boxers and curled her hand around his shaft. Trey's eyes were focused on her every move, which only made her want to please him more.

"Kiara, you don't have to…" His voice trailed off the moment Kiara's lips touched him. *Good*, she thought. *I can't be the only one being brought to my knees in pleasure.* Since the start of their trip, Trey had done anything he could to make sure she felt sexually satis-fied, and it was past time that she returned the favor.

His groans were like music to her ears as she used her mouth and hands to set a nice rhythm in her pur-suit to please him orally in a way she hoped he'd never been before.

Between the sound of the water and the sounds Trey was making, it was all the motivation Kiara needed to increase the movement of her tongue. A couple of minutes later, she could feel Trey's entire body tens-ing beneath her.

"Kiara, I'm close," he said. Instead of backing down, she increased her rhythm. Trey said her name twice more as a warning, but she didn't care. There was no way she was stopping. Seconds later, Trey's entire body convulsed as he released an orgasm that caused him to lightly grip the back of Kiara's head. Despite his previous warnings, Kiara didn't release him from her mouth until she was sure he'd released every last drop.

When she looked up into his face, the look of satisfaction she saw reflected in his eyes was exactly the look she'd been waiting for.

"You're amazing," Trey said, lightly touching her cheek. "Maybe one of these days we'll do something sexual in an actual bed."

"Or not." Kiara winked. "Beds are overrated. Maybe we should see how many more times we can have sex on anything other than a bed?"

The sly smile on his face was all the confirmation she needed. They only had a couple of days left of their trip, and Kiara planned on taking advantage of every moment.

Chapter 15

"Let me get this straight," Kyra said. "You had sex in a lifeguard stand in the middle of a tropical storm, but your knees are all scraped up because you decided to pleasure him on some rocks in a cave?"

Kiara rolled her eyes. "When I agreed to meet you for lunch, I didn't think the only thing we would talk about was my sex life."

Kyra waved her hand. "Girl, please. The fact that you have a sex life now is definitely worth an emergency lunch. You'd been back for an entire day and hadn't called to give me the details."

Kiara laughed. "Even so, you can't start making assumptions based on the few things I tell you. I didn't mention anything about scraping my knees on rocks."

"You didn't have to," Kyra said, after taking a sip of

her water. "You walked into the café limping on one leg and I can tell through your dress pants that you have gauze pads on your knees. I assume you did too much damage to cover it with a Band-Aid."

Kiara shook her head at how accurate Kyra was. To say her extended weekend with Trey was amazing would be a huge understatement. Right before they'd left the cave, he'd noticed her knees were bloodied from the rock. Apparently, it hadn't been as smooth as they'd thought. She'd been so wrapped up in the moment she hadn't even felt the pain.

Their descent down the Southern Alps had been a little tricky with her scraped knees, but eventually, they'd made it down safely, and back to the villa. Trey had catered to her the rest of the time and had been extra careful whenever they had sex after that. However, they'd kept their promise and had yet to have sex in a bed. It was almost a travesty to leave such a grand canopy bed like the one in the villa untouched, but Kiara liked the idea of them being unconventional. It was never a word she would have used to describe herself, but around Trey, she was learning to expect the unexpected.

"Okay, I've lost you again," Kyra said, breaking her thoughts. "Listen, you don't have to tell me any more sex details, but can we at least talk about what this means for the two of you?"

As if they spoke him up, Kiara received an incoming call from Trey. Kyra motioned for her to answer it.

"Hi, Trey," she said, ignoring the quirked eyebrow from Kyra.

"Hey, beautiful," Trey said. "How's your day going so far?"

"It's going okay. I'm having lunch with Kyra."

"That's nice. Tell her I said hi." Kiara exchanged pleasantries between the two.

"I don't want to keep you long, but there is a reason I called. Are you free tomorrow after work?"

"For a date?" she asked.

"Yes and no," Trey said. "I'm working on this huge project for Prescott George and I could really use your opinion on a few things. Do you think you could meet me someplace tomorrow after work? I'll even cook dinner for you later and change the bandages on your knees."

"How can a woman say no to that," Kiara said with a laugh. "Sure. Just text me the address of where we are meeting."

"Great—I will. Can't wait to see you."

"I can't wait to see you, either. 'Bye, Trey." Kiara disconnected the call with Trey and glanced at her phone.

"You can stare at your phone all day, but he's not in there, you know," Kyra said.

"I know that," Kiara said, lightly swatting at Kyra. "I was just thinking about how five weeks ago, you couldn't have told me I would be falling for a man like Trey Moore. Hell, you couldn't have even told me I'd be dating, period."

"That's the best way for it to work," Kyra said. "The best relationships happen when you aren't searching for one. Trey may not have been in your plans, but that dude is here to stay. I have a good feeling about him, Kiara. He's a good one."

"He is." *Maybe a little too good.* Did Kiara think that she deserved happiness? Of course. Did she think Trey could provide her with the type of relationship she'd always wanted? Absolutely. Did she think that her relationship with Trey was a little too good to be true? Unfortunately, yes. No matter how much she enjoyed the time she was spending with Trey, there was still the elephant in the room. Better yet, there was an elephant in her heart and she had to be honest with him eventually.

Their vacation in the French Riviera hadn't been the right time to tell him. Tomorrow may not be the right time, either. However, sooner or later, she'd have to stop making excuses and start telling him the truth. Her mother always reminded her that honesty was the best policy. She just hoped that honesty didn't result in heartbreak for her.

"I think the house looks pretty clean," Trey said as he glanced around the first level of his home. "What do you think, M-dog?" As usual, the baby cooed as he played with a toy in his playpen. "I'll take that as a yes."

Trey kept a clean home and the only time it truly got messy was when he was on a deadline. Even though the house wasn't exactly dirty, he'd needed to do some cleaning since he and M-dog had left the living room a bit untidy as they got back into a routine after he'd arrived back in the States.

Trey's vacation to the French Riviera had been everything he'd hoped it would be and more. His relationship with Kiara had really grown during the extended weekend, and their vacation would be marked as one of his favorite trips to his villa for years to come.

Trey folded the blanket at the corner of his sofa and laid it neatly across the back of the couch. He glanced down at M-dog. "I can't believe I'm cleaning my home for these knuckleheads."

He'd briefly seen his brother Derek when he'd picked up his nephew a couple of days ago, but their visit had been cut short when Derek had gotten an unexpected guest. Trey had asked for both Derek and Max to stop over tonight. He wasn't really surprised by how much he was looking forward to their visit. Even though they had to discuss Reginald's business, he wanted to catch up with them.

The doorbell rang, signaling their arrival. "Hey, fellas," he said when he opened the door to Derek and Max. "Thanks for stopping by after work. Did you both come together?"

"Nah," Derek said. "We happened to arrive at the same time." Derek looked past Trey to the playpen. "Hey, M-dog," he said as he lifted him in his arms. "How's my favorite little guy doing?"

"I bet he missed me more," Max said. "Isn't that right, M-dog?"

Trey laughed. "I take it that you both didn't have a problem watching him while I was away."

Both brothers nodded in agreement and Trey motioned for them to take a seat on the couch while he sat in his chair. They spent the next ten minutes discussing how easy Matthew had been to babysit while Trey was out of town.

"Man, don't keep us in suspense," Max said after a while. "How was your trip with Kiara?"

Trey sighed. "My trip with Kiara was amazing. We really needed this vacation to move our relationship forward, so I appreciate you both for suggesting the trip and watching M-dog for me."

"Don't mention it," Derek said. "We're just glad it worked out for you. Although that sappy smile you were wearing when you opened the door was enough to let us know that you enjoyed yourself."

Trey's smile grew even wider as he reflected on their trip. Although he hated that Kiara had bruised and cut her knees in the natural pool, the entire weekend with her had been memorable. He was already falling for her before they went out of town together, and now that they'd returned, he was pretty sure he was falling even harder and much faster than before.

"You're whipped," Max said, interrupting his thoughts.

"Damn right." Trey glanced outside his front window as he imagined all the times he'd opened that door to her beautiful, smiling face. "I'm not trying to sound cocky, but that woman is consuming my thoughts, so she might as well get *Mrs. Trey Moore* tattooed on her ring finger now." He looked up in time to see his brothers exchange a knowing look.

"Enough about me," Trey said. "Did anything happen with the investigation while I was gone? I haven't had a chance to contact Pete and figured I'd get an update from you guys today anyway."

Max cleared his throat. "Well, as much as we'd hoped to have better news for you when you got back from vacation, unfortunately, we don't."

"Do you remember the security guard who quit the San Diego chapter right after the break-in when those historic artifacts were stolen from their chapter headquarters?" Derek asked.

Trey nodded. "Yes, I remember."

"It turns out that he's talking now," Derek said. "He reached out to the San Diego board and told them that his life had been threatened, so he'd been too afraid to speak out a few months ago. But now he's admitting that he briefly saw the man who hit him over the head before stealing the artifacts."

"Let me guess," Trey said, shaking his head. "He's saying it's Reginald?"

"Sure is," Derek said. "Although I can't say I'm surprised." Trey wasn't surprised, either. Just disappointed.

"Reginald could still be innocent," Max said. "I believe my father when he says he wasn't behind this."

"I know you want to," Trey said. "Hell, Reginald had us all a little convinced he didn't have anything to do with the whole thing. Yet everything we've found so far makes him seem guilty."

"We still don't know who hired the hackers," Max said. "Pete said a couple of days ago that he needed more time to track down Insenia, the dark web group."

Trey glanced at Derek before they both looked at Max. "I understand that, Max. But at some point, you have to prepare yourself for the fact that at the end of our investigation, Reginald may still be found guilty."

"I know that," Max said. "And I'm prepared for that outcome. But I also think that the two of you have to keep an open mind throughout this process. If Reginald was framed like he says he was, all the evidence has been planted to make sure he stays guilty. If finding him innocent was going to be easy, he wouldn't have needed us to investigate in the first place."

Trey sighed as he let Max's words sink in. For a while the brothers sat in silence, each wrapped up in their own contemplations.

"Did you both give any additional thought to attending Thanksgiving next month at Reginald's home?" Max asked, breaking the silence.

Derek huffed. "Dining with the enemy and the man who's never been there for us? Why would we do that?"

"Because he's dying," Max said, unable to keep the emotion out of his voice. "I know he's never done anything but make both of your lives miserable, but I'm torn between the fact that I do care for my father and the fact that I'm getting to know brothers that I'd always hoped I'd be close to one day. I'm trying to make everyone happy, but I'm in a sticky situation."

"We're not telling you not to go," Trey said. "We'd never do that. But I feel the same way Derek does. I'm not turning down his invitation yet, but I need some more time to think about it."

"That's fair," Max said. The silence in the room returned, forcing Trey to observe each of his brothers and their current situation a little more.

"Listen," Trey said. "We knew that working together on this wasn't going to be easy and we were going to have different opinions about Reginald throughout this investigation. But I think the one thing we can all agree on is that we're forming a brotherhood that is decades too late. No matter what we discover, let's remember that the best thing about this request from Reginald is that the three of us have gotten closer. All three of us are even more active in Prescott George than we've ever been and I'm proud of us for not letting the rumors and accusations affect our character. Reginald may have given us the Moore last name, but the legacy is ours to change for the positive. We have the ability to leave our Moore mark on Prescott George and I say that we do everything in our power to make it an influential mark."

Derek laughed. "Powerful words from a powerful screenwriter. I can agree to that."

Max smiled. "Me, too."

"Glad to hear it." Trey stood from the chair. "Can't believe it took me this long to offer you a couple Coronas, so I'll grab them now."

"When you get back, let's change the subject," Derek suggested. "Maybe tell us more details about your vacation with the future Mrs. Trey Moore."

Trey popped the caps off the beers and returned to the living room. "Nah, I'm not about to be the only one talking about my love life. What about the two of you? Any future Mrs. Derek Moore or future Mrs. Max Moore that you care to share with the group?"

Derek busied himself with playing with M-dog while Max glanced up at the ceiling.

"It's like that?" Trey asked.

"Yup," Derek said.

Max nodded. "Pretty much."

"Fine, then," Trey said with a laugh. "Keep your secrets, for now." Trey turned on his television and chose the first sports game he could find. Before long, they were placing bets on which team would win, and the stress of the case was temporarily forgotten.

Chapter 16

"Bingo," Kiara said as she found a parking spot much closer to the basketball courts at Venice Beach than she'd expected to. *The parking gods must be on my side lately, because I've been finding space everywhere I go.* In a place as crowded as LA, Kiara had learned to cherish the little achievements.

As she stepped out of her car and made her way to the courts, she took a deep breath to calm her racing heart. It had been three days since she'd seen Trey and to say she missed him would be a huge understatement. She wasn't sure she'd even gone a full minute since their vacation without thinking about him.

When the lit courts came into view, Kiara spotted Trey and Matthew in his car seat right away. "Hey, Matthew," she said as she kissed his cheek before greeting Trey.

"I missed you," she said, surprised by her own honesty.

"I missed you, too." Trey lightly touched her hair, which she'd French-braided into one ponytail. "I love your hair."

"Thanks," she said. The words barely left her mouth before Trey pulled her to him with his free arm and kissed her senseless. *God, I've missed his lips.* Kiara would be the first to admit that she'd always enjoyed kissing, but she'd never felt like she *craved* kissing. The more time she spent with Trey, the more she craved his seductive kisses. A few catcalls from strangers caused them to break their kiss.

"The game already started," he said, pointing to the court. "I reserved a couple of chairs in the corner in front of the first row of bleachers."

Once they took their chairs, Kiara noticed that instead of jerseys, the teams playing basketball were wearing different colored T-shirts. "Do you know any of the kids playing tonight?" she asked.

"I know all of them," Trey said with a smile. "I'm heavily involved in Prescott George's community outreach, and all the kids playing tonight are part of the inner-city youth center downtown, where I regularly volunteer."

Kiara smiled. "That's awesome. I didn't know you volunteered at the youth center."

"Any chance I get. The holidays are always rough for a lot of the kids, so I'm usually there a couple of times a week this time of year. I hope you don't mind, but I wanted you to check out one of their games and to ask your advice."

Kiara shook her head. "Of course I don't mind. I'm honored that you thought of me. And I must admit, I'm surprised the kids have the entire court to themselves. Venice Beach courts are usually packed."

"One night a month, I reserve these courts for the youth center," Trey said. "That way, the kids can get out of their normal routine for a little while."

"So you write award-winning screenplays. On a good night, you can cook a mean meal. Your idea of sweeping a woman off her feet isn't tickets to a Broadway musical, but rather, taking her on a private jet to an exotic location. You dote on your adorable nephew. And just in case anyone suspected that you weren't as great as you sound, you regularly volunteer with the local inner-city youth, which includes getting for them an entire extremely well-known basketball court one night a month so they can play without interruption." Kiara couldn't contain the smile that crossed her face. "I can't imagine there is anything you can't do."

"That's not true," Trey said with a laugh. "I've written plenty of screenplays that haven't won awards. I don't sweep women off their feet—only one woman who's managed to capture my complete and undivided attention because she's much more amazing than she realizes. I may be taking care of M-dog now, but we both know he was running the show in the beginning. And while I can't imagine not volunteering at the youth center and working with some amazing kids, there are plenty of things I can't do. Like fly. Or parallel park in LA."

Kiara laughed so hard she made a couple of young girls sitting close by them jump in their seats a little. "You can't parallel park?"

"I never said I couldn't parallel park at all," Trey said. "I just can't park in LA. If they don't have a parking lot, I usually have my driver take me there. I've hit one too many cars in the past trying to park."

Kiara shook her head. "I'm teaching you to park."

Trey gave her a Chuck E. Cheese smile. "I was hoping you'd take pity on me."

"You're ridiculous," Kiara said, rolling her eyes. She glanced back out at the court. "You mentioned needing my advice about something earlier. What did you need help with?"

"Well, it's no secret that I'm completely impressed with what you've done at LA Little Ones."

"Thank you," she said with a smile.

"You're welcome." Trey waved at some kids who called out his name from a few rows above them. "I've been working with the youth center for years and Prescott George has successfully implemented several programs geared toward helping the elementary and high school groups. That includes after-school tutoring, career development and informational meetings on furthering their education. The issue that I'm running into is developing an early education program to target the younger kids. So, I thought that maybe you could interact with some of the kids tonight and at another event and give me some ideas for the program."

Kiara clapped her hands together. "I would love to help. We've had lots of success with the programs we've created at LA Little Ones, and I've already talked to the staff about possibly streamlining those programs to an even slightly higher age group than we currently target. I could share some of our findings, and then we could see if they would work with your plans."

Instead of responding to her right away, Trey leaned in and placed a soft kiss on her lips. "Thank you," he said before he went in for a second and third kiss.

"Eww," a voice said from behind them. "Mr. Trey is sucking that woman's face off." Kiara broke the kiss and tried to cover her laugh.

"This is grown folks' business," Trey said.

"You're in public," the other girl said. "So it's everybody's business."

Kiara gave up trying to hold in her laugh and turned to the girls. "Hello. My name is Kiara. What's your names?"

"I'm Daja," one said with a smile.

"I'm Tatiana," the other said. "And we really like your hair. I wish my hair could do that." Tatiana ran her fingers over her thick head of hair.

"You can," Kiara said. "My hair is thick like yours and I didn't know how to braid it when I was your age. Someone had to teach me."

"Could you teach me?" Tatiana asked in an excited voice.

"Sure," Kiara said. "But for now, how about I braid your hair, and then next time I see you, I'll show you how?"

Tatiana turned to Trey. "Will you promise to bring her to the center, Mr. Trey?"

Trey laughed. "I will."

Kiara stood. "If you scoot over a little, I'll sit next to you and braid your hair." Tatiana anxiously scooted over, and even Daja seemed excited to watch Kiara braid her friend's hair. Kiara didn't have an actual comb, so she had to finger-comb Tatiana's hair first. Except for her nieces, Kiara couldn't remember the last time she'd braided hair. She was so wrapped up in the moment that she hadn't noticed the way Trey was intently watching her over his shoulder.

When she smiled at him, she swore his look only intensified. She was about to make a joke and ask him if she had something on her face, until her mind recalled that the last time she'd seen that look in his eyes had been when he was talking about his nephew while they were in the French Riviera. She'd seen it again when she'd arrived at the basketball court tonight and he was talking about the youth center.

It was the look of a man who was realizing that she'd make a good mother. She'd seen the look before in her husband and she'd seen it again in her last boyfriend. Kiara broke eye contact with Trey and continued braiding Tatiana's hair. Although she wanted to ignore the feeling in the pit of her stomach, she knew she couldn't overlook the inevitable any longer. *He deserves to know the truth, so tonight you must be open and honest with him.*

There was a strong chance she'd lose Trey the same way she'd lost her exes, but it was only fair to let him know what he was getting himself into before it was too late. As she swallowed back her nerves, the rational side of her knew that it already was.

"Are you sure you're okay?" Trey asked.

Kiara smiled, but Trey thought the smile didn't quite reach her eyes. "I'm fine. Tonight was a lot of fun."

After the basketball game, Trey and Kiara had hung out with the kids from the youth center for another half hour. The kids all loved Kiara, but Trey hadn't been surprised. In his experience with her, there wasn't anyone she met who didn't enjoy being around her.

After, he'd asked Kiara if she still wanted to continue the night back at his place. She'd teased him about the fact that he'd only driven himself to Venice Beach because they had a couple of parking lots, but luckily, she agreed.

When Trey approached his front door, he knew his sister, Carmen, had arrived before he'd even unlocked it. More lights were on than when he'd left and she was the only one who always locked the top lock, but never the bottom. A quick glance at his street proved she'd parked a few houses down.

"This is unexpected," Trey said to Kiara as he opened the top lock. "My sister is here. She must have gotten a short break from filming her television series."

Kiara looked surprised, but only smiled. Trey was prepared for his sister's usually bubbly personality, but that was not the trait that greeted him when they walked into his home.

"So glad you're home," Carmen said, standing from

the couch. She raced over to them and picked up Matthew from his car seat. "Oh, my sweet boy, I missed you so much." She cradled Matthew to her chest and the baby cooed in excitement at seeing his mom.

"Carmen, what's wrong?" Her cheeks were still wet from freshly fallen tears.

Carmen turned to Trey. "I'm so sorry to stop by like this, but they cut my role. After more than two weeks of filming, they cut the role without giving it a second thought."

"I'm so sorry, Carmen," Trey said, pulling her in for a hug, careful not to crush Matthew. "The right role will come along. It just means this wasn't meant to be."

His sister grew silent and Trey realized that she'd finally noticed Kiara was standing behind him. "How rude of me," Carmen said, glancing at Kiara apologetically. She extended her hand to Kiara. "I'm Trey's sister, Carmen."

"It's nice to meet you," Kiara said, taking her hand. "I'm Kiara." She turned to Trey. "How about I wait in the kitchen and let the two of you talk."

Carmen gave her a grateful smile, and even though they had only just met, Kiara placed a supportive hand on Carmen's forearm before she left for the kitchen.

"I've ruined your night," Carmen said as they walked back to the couch. "I should have called you the minute I found out."

Trey shook his head. "You didn't ruin anything. You're my sister. Anytime you need me, I'm here."

Carmen glanced down at Matthew's smiling face.

"He looks so happy. Thank you so much for taking care of him."

"M-dog and I have gotten really close, haven't we, M-dog?" Matthew blew a spit bubble that caused them both to laugh.

"Is Kiara the same Kiara that owns LA Little Ones?" Carmen asked. Trey had always kept his sister up to date with Matthew's whereabouts when he wasn't with him.

"Yes, that's her."

"I see," Carmen said with a knowing smile. "You left out the part where she's extremely beautiful, but I should have known that was the case when you mentioned going out of town with her."

"My bad," Trey said. "Kiara is the woman who's been helping me with M-dog and keeping me sane these past few weeks. She is as beautiful as she is intelligent."

"Wow," Carmen said. "Big words from my brother. And how does she feel about the nickname M-dog?"

Trey laughed. "She hates it."

Carmen placed a hand over her chest. "A woman after my own heart. Okay, now I need all the details. Tell me exactly how you met."

Trey spent the next few minutes giving Carmen the condensed version of his relationship with Kiara so far. Just as she began telling him about the good times she had filming the pilot, her phone pinged, interrupting their conversation. "I just received an email from your brother Max." A smile crossed her face. "Looks like I landed an audition for another television series tomorrow."

"That's great," Trey said. "Another pilot?"

"Nope. This is a medical show that's been on a main network station for years." Carmen scrolled through some additional details on her phone. "I think I have a chance at getting the part."

"Of course you do," Trey said. "You can do anything you set your mind to." Even though Max had a responsibility to Carmen as her talent agent, Trey made a mental note to call Max later and thank him for finding something for her so quickly.

Carmen smiled. "Thanks, big brother! Now, how about Matthew and I get out of your way so you can continue your date."

Trey glanced down at Matthew before looking toward the kitchen. "I'm going to miss M-dog, but I'm anxious to get my girl all alone."

Carmen's eyes widened. "Dare I say my big brother is falling in love?"

Trey shrugged. "You can say that." He hadn't been prepared for her high-pitched squeal, but all he could do was laugh. Moments later, Carmen packed up a few of Matthew's things and said goodbye to Kiara.

"I'll pick up everything else sometime this week," Carmen said as Trey helped her to her car. "Go enjoy your night."

Once Carmen and Matthew were gone, Trey knew he had approximately twenty-four hours before Carmen was going to contact his mom while she was on her African safari and tell her all about him and Kiara.

Trey walked to the kitchen with an extra pep in his step, ready to see what the rest of the night had in store.

However, the moment his eyes landed on Kiara, he knew a carefree night wasn't in their near future.

"We need to talk," she said, a seriousness in her eyes that he hadn't seen before. As Trey stood there observing her behavior, he thought back to all the screenplays he'd written with scenes such as this one. Anytime he wrote, his entire objective was to place himself in the character's position to get a better understanding of how they would handle a situation. Whether it was real life or fictional life, no man ever wanted to hear the words *We need to talk* come out of a woman's mouth.

Chapter 17

Kiara took another sip of her water, her nerves getting the best of her. She knew she'd caught Trey off guard when he'd entered his kitchen, evident in the fact that he stood for a few seconds simply staring at her. Finally, he poured himself a glass of water and took a seat across from her.

"What's going on?" Trey asked, concern engraved in his eyes. As much as she wished she could wipe that look off his face, she couldn't. *Tonight, you tell him everything. Don't chicken out.*

"I wanted to talk to you about my divorce." Kiara took a deep breath. "I'm finally ready to tell you about it."

Trey nodded in understanding. "I'm all ears."

Taking another deep breath, Kiara racked her brain

on where to start. *Goodness, his eyes are sexy.* Trey had the type of piercing eyes that could bring a woman to her knees. They were so warm and hypnotizing that she almost wanted to take back the fact that she'd started this conversation. *Almost.*

"I guess you could say on the outside, looking in, that Jerry and I had a great relationship. We were both successful in our careers and we had our entire future planned out."

"How long were you married?"

"For two years," Kiara said. "We'd been dating for three years prior to that, so we were together for five years totally." She grew quiet as she thought about some of the good times they'd had before everything had turned sour. "You see, I may be the type of person who likes to have a plan, but Jerry was much worse than I was. His timeline was much stricter and it was something that hadn't bothered me at all in the beginning."

"Until it did," Trey said.

Kiara nodded. "Yes, until it did. First, I noticed that he'd had these ideals that I hadn't really detected before. I'd wanted to start LA Little Ones for as long as I could remember, but I soon realized that Jerry didn't really want a wife to run her own business. He wanted her to be the housewife type."

Trey frowned. "Only weak-minded men think about limiting their partner's potential with unidealistic and sexist views."

God, he's amazing. "I agree," Kiara said. "I obviously didn't listen to his crazy notions, but I wish I had seen them for what they were. They were a sign that when faced with life-changing issues, Jerry was not going to be the type of man to stay by my side."

Kiara took another sip of her water. "Our true problems started a month into our marriage when Jerry wanted us to try and have our first child. According to his timeline, he needed to have one child before a large case he was working on was solved that would result in him being partner of his law firm."

Trey's eyes widened. "Your ex-husband is Jerry Bishop? The one who won that politician's case?"

"Unfortunately," she said with a nod. "Since his career has taken off in the past couple years, I'm assuming you've heard of him."

"I have," Trey said. "Word is, he's also been trying to join Prescott George, but the board isn't having it. Something about him rubbing some of the LA chapter members the wrong way."

"He has that effect on people. Luckily, we divorced before he became too well-known. Our divorce was clean considering how things could have gone down."

"That's good to hear," Trey said. "I assume that since you've told me that you don't want to have kids, that was part of the issue when Jerry decided he wanted to try and have your first child?"

Kiara sighed. "Not exactly. Back then, I wanted kids more than I wanted my next breath." She tried to disregard the way Trey's lips curled to the side in a hopeful smile, but it was impossible to ignore. "Starting a family right away was a plan Jerry and I had in common."

"I had a feeling you wanted kids," Trey said. "You're way too good with kids not to be a mother."

Kiara winced at his statement. "I'll never deny that, back then, I wanted kids and I wanted to be a mother. But I quickly learned that, sometimes, we can't always get what we want." *Just rip off the Band-Aid, Kiara. It will make the rest of your conversation a lot easier.* She clammed up, her mind racing with flashbacks of what she'd gone through and flash-forwards of a life she'd never have.

She wasn't sure when Trey had reached across the table and taken her hand in his, but she had to admit she appreciated the comfort.

Leaning slightly forward and holding back tears she refused to let fall, she forced herself to get the words out. "It's not that I don't want kids, Trey. I would love to have a child of my own one day, but according to every doctor and specialist I saw back then, having children was never a possibility for me."

Based on the combined look of pity and concern reflected in his eyes, she knew he'd finally understood what she'd been trying to say. She didn't want his pity, but that was always the first reaction she received from people when they found out.

"Physically, I can never have kids," she continued. "And as much as I wish that weren't the case, it is. I had every test known to man, and the last year of my marriage, any hope was taken away from me when I experienced some unexpected bleeding and had to have an emergency hysterectomy. That surgery sealed my fate, which meant there was no way I'd be able to bear children because of it."

Kiara's heart was beating so fast she felt like it was

in her throat. "I don't know how to explain it, but for any woman to lose a part of herself that is uniquely female and for the sole purpose of bearing children is a tough pill to swallow. For years, it made me feel like less of a person. I wouldn't wish that type of pain on any woman."

Trey lifted her hand to his lips and placed a soft kiss on each of her fingers. "I am so sorry you had to go through that. I can't imagine how you felt having to overcome those obstacles."

"It wasn't easy," she said. "And it still isn't easy. But it's my story whether I want to rewrite those chapters or not. As much as I hate that I'll never have my own children, what hurts most of all is that I can't even blame the men I dated for leaving me. My ex-husband left me because of it. My last boyfriend didn't propose because of it." *And if history is indeed repeating itself, you'll realize I'm not worth it, too.*

Kiara had always prided herself on being able to overcome her fears, but sitting at the table, talking to Trey about her least favorite topic in the entire world, was causing her fears to wash over her in waves.

That was not what I expected her to say. Trey had always been wordy. A trait that he admired since it helped him in his career as screenwriter. However, sitting across from Kiara and hearing her recount the details of one of the hardest experiences of her life, he couldn't find the words.

He'd known that whatever Kiara had been hesitating on telling him was something big, but he'd had no idea that she'd been keeping this to herself for as long as she had. Granted, they hadn't known each other for a long time, but in the time they'd spent together, she'd become one of the most important people in his life.

Trey scooted his chair around the table so that he was sitting beside Kiara. Her eyes were watery and he felt like, any moment, she'd release the tears she'd been fighting to keep at bay. There were so many emotions Trey was feeling while he listened to Kiara, and he wasn't sure which emotion to act on first.

"Kiara," he said, opting to comfort her and take the pain away first. "You said once that you feared that what you had to tell me would result in my feelings changing for you. Is this what you were afraid to tell me?"

She nodded. "Yes, it is."

He gripped her hands even tighter in his. "Then, baby, let me state for the record that I am not your ex-husband, nor am I your ex-boyfriend. Although it breaks my heart to hear about everything you've gone through, learning that you can't have children doesn't change the way I feel about you."

"How can you say that?" Kiara asked, wiping away a tear. "I've seen how you are with Matthew, and I've seen the way you look at the kids in the youth center. You want to be a father, Trey. You want to have kids of your own."

Trey shook his head. "I've told you before that having kids of my own was never really something I considered before. Yes, I adore my nephew and the kids in the youth center, but I adore you even more, Kiara. In case you haven't realized it, you're my future."

By now, Kiara's tears were starting to fall down her cheeks, and Trey wished he could take away every negative feeling she had about their future together. "Trey, you don't know what you're saying. You don't understand the risks you'd be taking by being with someone like me. It's easy to say you don't want kids now, but what about five years from now? Or ten years from now? What happens when we're old and gray and you start to have these regrets about the life you could have had with a woman who could give you everything you want?"

"Baby, you are everything I want." Trey cupped her face in his hands, brushing away her tears with his fingertips. "When I think about my future and the life that I want, you are the only person I see. Kiara, I'm not perfect. No one is. As individuals, we are more than the burdens that are placed upon us, and, sweetie, when I look into your eyes, all I see is the woman who has captured my heart. A woman who is as beautiful and kind on the inside as she is on the outside."

Trey placed a soft kiss on her lips. "Maybe you were given this burden because you have way too much love to give and bestow upon other children. Your business is a prime example of how much better the LA youth are because they have a person like you in their lives."

The room grew silent for a few seconds, but Trey noticed that Kiara's tears seemed to be subsiding. "If you decide to be with me, I think you may regret it," she said, her voice barely above a whisper.

Trey lifted her eyes to his, determined to make her see what he felt in his heart. "Kiara, I will never regret being with you. When I fell in love with you, I fell in love with all of you. My love isn't circumstantial."

Her eyes widened at his submission, and all Trey wanted to do was continue to prove to her that what they had could withstand any obstacles. Within seconds, he'd lifted her from her chair and picked her up in his arms.

"Where are we going?" she asked, her eyes filling with desire.

"I figure it's past time for me to make love to you in a proper bed." Her response was a kiss that he felt all the way down to his toes.

Once they were in his bedroom, he placed her gently in the middle of the bed and began removing her clothes. "I want you to try and relax," Trey said when he tossed her bra and panties aside to join everything else he'd removed.

Next, he took off his own clothes and smiled when he noticed even more of the tension releasing from her body. He went to join her on the bed.

"The sooner you realize you can't get rid of me, the easier it will be for you," he said, placing kisses along her body. She laughed, and not long after, her laughter turned to sweet moans that were slowly becoming his favorite melody.

He'd meant everything he'd told her tonight. He'd fallen in love with her, and the quicker she got used to the idea, the easier it would be. He had to admit that a part of his heart had broken when Kiara had told him about her inability to have kids, but it wasn't for the reasons she'd assumed. Trey knew that he and Kiara would be okay. As a matter of fact, he was sure of it. However, he hated that she'd gone through what she had on her own, because from the sound of it, Jerry wasn't a man at all. Neither was her other ex.

"Relax," Trey whispered in her ear before he kissed a couple of scars on her stomach that he now understood held more meaning than he'd ever thought before. "The men in your past never deserved you." He kissed her inner thighs. "A woman like you should never feel as though she is less...only more." Trey dipped his tongue in her center and was rewarded by her bucking off the bed.

He placed his hand around her legs and brought her closer to his mouth. He'd been craving her taste since the last time he'd tasted her, and tonight, he wanted nothing more than to bring her the utmost pleasure.

Kiara moved her hips to the stroke of his tongue, and moments later, Trey felt the buildup of her orgasm.

"I need you," Kiara said breathlessly, her hips still meeting his tongue. "I need you inside me *right now.*"

He reached for a foil packet in his nightstand, but Kiara pushed his hands away.

"I trust you and I need to feel you without it," she said. When he noticed the worry lines return to her face as a reminder of their serious conversation, he went back to work on making her forget all her worries.

Trey rolled his tongue around her nub a few more times before he felt her shatter beneath his mouth. Only then did he remove his mouth and ease himself inside while she was still convulsing as her orgasm neared its end. The moment he was embedded fully inside, they both released a sigh of satisfaction.

"I love you," Trey said as he began moving his hips to the rhythm they were getting familiar with. "Never forget that. You're not alone anymore. I'll be by your side through anything life throws our way." She nodded her head, before tossing it into the sheets as he increased the movement of his hips.

Trey knew the night had been an emotional roller coaster for Kiara, but he didn't need her to say the words back just yet. Deep down in his heart, he knew she felt the same way. And after tonight, he would do everything he could to make sure she never forgot just how much she meant to him.

Chapter 18

I need to be sure that this relationship is something I want. Please give me a week to think and figure out some things.

For the past three days, Trey had reflected on the words Kiara had told him during their last conversation, which meant he still had four more days left before he could see her or talk to her.

Trey pulled at his cell phone and scrolled through his photos until he found the picture he'd taken of Kiara on the balcony of his villa when they'd been on vacation. He'd taken a lot more photos that weekend, but this one was by far his favorite. She looked so carefree in the photo. Not a worry in the world.

Trey was less than thrilled about Kiara's request for space, but he understood that the fears she had were a result of what she'd been through in prior relationships. Even though he knew he'd never leave her, Kiara had to come to terms with it. Otherwise, their relationship would never work. Just in case she needed an additional reminder that giving her space didn't mean he was giving up on them, he texted her every morning to let her know she was always in his heart.

A call on his cell replaced the photo on his iPhone screen. "What's up, Max?"

"It's Reginald. His health has taken a turn for the worse. Can you meet me at the mansion in an hour? Derek's on his way, too."

Trey frowned. Just yesterday, Max had texted him and Derek that Reginald was having a good day. Apparently, that had been short-lived. "Sure. I'll be there soon."

As soon as he disconnected the call, he saw an incoming call from Pete. "Hey, Pete. Tell me you have good news."

"Some good news. Some bad news," Pete said. "You ready?"

"Shoot."

Trey talked to Pete and got the recent details on his findings. Although Trey would have liked for more concrete information, he was appreciative of what Pete was able to find.

An hour later, Trey, Max and Derek stood in Reginald's massive bedroom while the nurse took his temperature.

"Why the gloomy faces?" Reginald asked. "Never seen a man dying before?"

"That's not funny," Max said. "You've got to slow down. Just because you have a good day doesn't mean you can overdo it. Otherwise, you end up bedridden for the next few days."

"I know, I know," Reginald said. "I promise to slow down."

Trey shuffled from one foot to the other as he observed his father. Growing up, he'd always thought of Reginald as someone larger than life, whether Trey liked him as a person or not. Seeing him look so helpless was difficult.

Reginald coughed a few times before the nurse informed them that he needed his rest.

"Before you leave," Reginald said. "Did you give more thought about my invitation to join me for Thanksgiving?"

Max looked at Trey and Derek, who shared a knowing look. Trey knew Derek didn't want anything to do with Reginald, but seeing him in such bad shape was a bit too much for either of them to handle.

"We'll be here for the holiday," Trey said with mixed emotions. With that, the three of them left the bedroom and walked down the hall to Reginald's office.

"I've got some news," Trey said. "Pete called me before I arrived and told me that he was able to locate the person from Insenia that was hired to hack into those San Diego files. Bad news, the hacker didn't have the name of the person who hired him. Good news, he was able to tell Pete that Reginald Moore wasn't the person who hired him, but rather, Reginald was part of the job he was hired for. The hacker was asked to leave clues in the coding that made it appear like Reginald was the one to log in and access those private files."

"You're kidding me," Derek said. "So, whoever hired him wanted Reginald to be framed just like Reginald believed."

Trey nodded. "It seems that way."

Max looked relieved. "I knew something good would turn up sooner or later. And that's not the only good news. I got a call from a friend in the San Diego chapter earlier this morning."

"What did he say?" Trey asked.

"It turns out that the security guard who came forward and accused Reginald of stealing the historic artifacts was actually the one behind the heist. Well, not him directly, but his nephew by marriage, who's a well-known thief in the San Diego area. I guess some of the San Diego board members suspected that his story didn't add up, and the security guard got nervous. He sang like a canary when the board asked him to come in for additional questioning."

Trey shook his head. "I can't believe they didn't look further into the security guard in the beginning."

"Me, neither," Max said. "I think the entire chapter was quick to put the blame on Reginald since he was already accused of so much. The San Diego chapter is going to reach out to the LA chapter later today, but I wanted you both to know before the news circulated within Prescott George."

Derek ran his fingers down his face. "This may be good news, but what do we do next? We still need more answers."

Trey looked from Derek to Max. "I say we continue with the investigation, but also make sure we keep most things we find between the three of us. Of course, we'll need to loop in some people, but we still don't know whom we can trust. And a couple of wins doesn't mean we've solved the entire case. Reginald was accused of quite a bit, so this may take a while."

Max and Derek nodded in agreement, and the men discussed their next steps. Two hours later, it wasn't lost on Trey that even though Reginald was resting, it was the longest he'd been within the same vicinity of all three sons in years.

"Open up this door right now, young lady. Your car is in the driveway, so I know you're here."

Kiara winced at the pounding on the other side of the door. She already knew it was her mom and she suspected she was stopping over to try to talk some sense into her.

Reluctantly, Kiara stood from her couch and went to open the door for Gina. "Mom, you shouldn't have cut your time short in Seattle just to come see me."

"Oh, hush, child," Gina said. "You know I had to come home to give your brother a piece of my mind. The only reason I'm here is because I could hear the stress in your voice and I didn't like it."

Kiara went to sit back down on her sofa. "Sorry you didn't like what you heard." Quite frankly, she didn't like how she'd sounded, either. Even though Kiara wasn't in the best state of mind, she could still appreciate her mother's flawless beauty. For a woman who'd had four children and was in her upper sixties, she didn't look a day over forty.

"What is it, sweet girl?" Gina asked, sitting beside her daughter. As she had so many times while Kiara was growing up, she reached for Kiara's head and leaned it against her chest. Kiara's arms reached around her mother's waist and the simple embrace was enough to cause Kiara's waterworks to flood her face.

"I don't know what's wrong with me," Kiara said. "I took your advice and told Trey everything. He knows the truth and that I do want children, but can't physically carry any children of my own."

"Oh, sweetie," Gina said. "Did he not take the news well?"

"Quite the opposite," Kiara said, wiping a few tears from her face. "He took the news better than I ever could have imagined." She spent the next few minutes telling her mother about her conversation with Trey and how special and attentive he'd been to her the rest of the night. She left out the part about him making love to her afterward.

After she was finished telling the story of how the night had unfolded, Kiara felt a wave of guilt over how she'd handled things with Trey the next morning.

"I think I messed up," Kiara said. "We'd had an amazing vacation, followed by a night filled with truth, hope and promise. Then the next morning, I got scared and told him that I need some time to figure out if this relationship is something I want." Kiara sighed. "How could I not see how selfish I was being?"

"Kiara, it takes a strong woman to tell the man she

loves a truth that could jeopardize their relationship, but you've already done the hard part," Gina said.

"I may have told him about not being able to bear children, but I haven't told him that I love him yet. Mom, he's done nothing but be sweet and supportive. I'm not even sure how to move forward with Trey."

Gina leaned Kiara forward so that she could look Kiara in the eyes. "I've always raised you to face your fears, but as your mother, I also realize that your childhood was robbed from you the minute your father walked out on us. I was the adult and I should have forced you to hold on to your childhood a little bit longer."

"No, Mom," Kiara said, shaking her head. "That wasn't your fault."

"You're right," Gina said. "Your father leaving us was nobody's fault but his own. However, since I had to work so many jobs to support you and your siblings, you were forced to run the household while I made enough money to pay the bills."

Kiara shook her head. "I didn't mind."

"I know you didn't," Gina said. "Kiara, you have always been nurturing and placed others' needs before your own. It's what makes you so special, but it's also what opens you up to being taken advantage of sometimes."

"You didn't take advantage of me." Kiara took her mom's hands in hers. "I was happy to do my part."

"You always were," Gina said, emotion filling her voice. "And even though I didn't want you to grow up so fast, I need you to understand that every morning I woke up ready to conquer whatever life threw my way was because I had an amazing daughter reminding me that, in her eyes, I was her superwoman."

Kiara sniffled. "You'll always be my superwoman."

She gave her mom a tight hug as they shed a few more tears. "Kiara, you've never had someone take care of you and treat you the way you deserve to be treated," Gina said. "I often prayed that you'd meet a man who knew your worth. And although I still want to meet Trey, I can already tell he sees my daughter for the wonderful person she is. Let him love you, Kiara. I know you've had a lot of bad things happen in your life, and it's expected for you to have some insecurities about relationships. Sweetie, any woman can be loved by a man. But to be loved by the *right* man is a different story entirely. Let go of your fears, sweetie. Let them go."

Kiara cried into her mother's hug, releasing more emotion than she had in years. It was just the right amount of mother-therapy that she needed to accept the fears she'd held on to for years and move forward from them.

Kiara and Gina sat quietly for a few moments before Kiara broke the silence. "He texts me every day just to let me know that he's thinking about me, he loves me and he's counting down the time until we can see each other again."

"I like him," Gina said with a laugh. "Have you given any more thought to when you're going to go talk to him?"

"I have an idea," Kiara said, wiping her face with the back of her hand and perking up in her seat. She'd spent the past few days wallowing in her insecurities, and she could only imagine how that made Trey feel. "Hopefully, after I put my plan into place, Trey will realize that not only do I love him, but I'll also never have doubts about his love for me again."

Gina smiled and lightly touched Kiara's cheek. "Go get your man, baby girl."

Chapter 19

Trey glanced around his home, realizing that it had never been as clean as it had looked the past week. *That's what happens when you have time on your hands and you're trying to give your woman the space she requested.*

He had gotten a call from his agent earlier this morning, and as he'd hoped, they were predicting that his latest screenplay could be up for Best Original Screenplay. Although Trey appreciated the great feedback, he knew the only reason he'd made it through that screenplay was because of a very sexy brown beauty who'd managed to steal his heart in a short amount of time.

His phone ringing interrupted his cleaning. "Hello, this is Trey Moore."

"Hello, Mr. Moore. This is Lacey, one of the bid assistants for Rent-a-Bachelor. We've spoken before."

Trey frowned. The last thing he wanted was to get rented right now. "Hi, Lacey. Yes, I remember speaking before. What can I do for you?"

"You've been rented again, sir. Are you free for the next five evenings?"

"Five evenings?" Trey asked. "I'm not sure I stated my availability to be open that long."

"You did, sir," Lacey said. "Need I remind you that the bidder placed a pretty penny for your time and you did have your calendar listed as free?"

Trey groaned into the phone although he hadn't meant to. He'd placed a hold of a week and a half on his calendar so he could finish his screenplay and go on his vacation with Kiara. He'd meant to adjust his availability after that time.

"We're only following the rules you created, sir," Lacey said. Trey almost laughed at the irony that even he—the creator of Rent-a-Bachelor—had to follow the rules. *Maybe I need to have this program reevaluated.*

"I understand, Lacey. Yes, I'm available."

"Great," she said. "You've been rented by Kiara Woods again."

Trey perked up. "Did you say Kiara Woods?"

"Yes, sir. Kiara Woods. Per her request, she asked that you meet at her place tonight."

After getting a couple of additional details, Trey disconnected the call, suddenly more excited for the day than he'd been all week.

Kiara wasn't sure there was ever a moment when she was as nervous as she was now. *All you have to do is make the call. No big deal.* Except, it was a huge deal. Everything about tonight mattered to Kiara and she wanted to make sure the night went smoothly.

Without giving it a second thought, she pulled out her cell phone and dialed the phone number. The recipient answered on the second ring.

"Hello?" the female voice asked.

Kiara took a deep breath. "Hello, Carmen. This is Kiara Woods. I received your phone number from Trey's friend Kendrick Burrstone. I hope it's okay that I'm calling you."

"Kiara, hi," Carmen said. "Of course it's fine that you called. Is everything okay?"

"Not really, but I'm hoping that after tonight, it will be. I know we met only briefly, but I really like your brother and I wanted to do something special for him. To do that, I need your help."

The other line grew silent, and Kiara worried that Trey had told his sister about the fact that Kiara had needed some time to think this past week.

"I've never had the strong feelings I have for Trey for any other man," Kiara said. "Some days ago, I told Trey I needed to do some thinking about our relationship, when I just hadn't fully faced my fears about caring so much for someone and having them not return those same feelings. Tonight, I really want Trey to realize that I'm in this for the long haul and I'm not going anywhere."

Carmen grew silent again. "Carmen, are you still there?"

"Sorry," Carmen said. "I was changing Matthew's

diaper when you called and this boy won't stay still for anything. I've been placing you on and off hold so that you don't hear the struggle, because let me tell you, Matthew is winning this war."

Kiara sighed in relief before laughing. *Okay, so the silence wasn't because of me.*

"My brother has dated some questionable women in his past, but I like you, Kiara," Carmen said. "And I've had my share of heartbreak, most recently from Matthew's father, so I understand your fears. I'm hoping that, with time, you and I can get closer and get to know one another. My brother means the world to me, and he deserves a woman like you who sees how amazing he is, so I'm all ears. What do you need my help with?"

Although Carmen couldn't see her, Kiara gave the biggest smile she'd given all day, before she proceeded to tell her the plan.

As Trey approached Kiara's home, he felt like a kid in a candy shop. He'd spent the entire day excited to see Kiara tonight, and he was anxious to know why she'd rented him for so many days after asking for some time to think.

He rang her doorbell and adjusted his blazer. He'd chosen to go semi-casual and wear jeans, a white T and a beige blazer, since he wasn't sure what Kiara had planned. He smiled when he thought about the fact that he'd also been able to see M-dog for a couple of hours after Carmen called and asked him to stop by her place and watch him for a little while. Trey had welcomed the distraction of his nephew. Otherwise, he could have been anxiously watching the clock as he waited for the time to pass until he got to see Kiara.

Trey glanced through Kiara's side window and noticed, for the first time, that no lights were on.

"That's strange," he said aloud. He was sure the bid assistant had informed him that Kiara wanted him to meet her at her home. A quick check of his email confirmation confirmed that he hadn't misunderstood.

Just as he rang the doorbell a second time, he noticed an envelope on the welcome mat with his name written on the outside. He'd been so preoccupied with seeing Kiara, he hadn't noticed it before. Trey opened the envelope and began reading.

Roses are red. Violets are blue.
Please visit the location where I first laid eyes
on you.
Love, Kiara.

Trey flipped the card over to see if anything else was written on it. "Seriously," he said aloud. "She's sending me on a wild-goose chase?" His question was answered when he rang the doorbell twice more and there was still no answer. All he could do was laugh and head to the first place he'd met Kiara. The LA Prescott George headquarters.

During the drive, Trey had to convince himself not to run any lights. He even called Kiara twice and she didn't answer, but texted him a kissing emoji. "That's fine," he said to himself. "I'll get her back when all of this is over." And he had the sweetest kind of payback in mind.

He arrived at the Fine Arts Building and made his

way to the twelfth-floor penthouse suite. Steve, the security officer, greeted him when he arrived.

"Hi, Steve."

"Hello, Trey." Steve reached in his back pocket and pulled out an envelope. "This is for you."

"Thank you." Trey smiled and shook his head as he opened the second envelope.

> *The beauty of the sunset.*
> *The lushness of a tree.*
> *When I rented this sexy man I met,*
> *I had no idea the impact he'd have on me.*
> *Love, Kiara.*

She's back at my place. He wasn't sure how he knew, but he did. Trey flipped over the card again, just as he had the first one, to make sure there wasn't anything else. Nodding goodbye to Steve, he made his way back to his house.

He arrived at his house and swung open the door, expecting to see her waiting in his living room, but she wasn't. He glanced around the room and spotted another envelope on his coffee table. Instead of another poem written on a card, she had written only two words.

Rooftop Terrace

Trey took the stairs two at a time, wearing the biggest smile he'd worn all week. Given everything that had been on his mind lately, he was ready to see his woman and make up for a week's worth of lost time.

* * *

Kiara knew the moment Trey had made it to his rooftop terrace, because she got goose bumps all over. When her eyes landed on his face, she breathed a sigh of relief. There was something in his eyes that put all her nerves at ease.

"I'm glad you found me," she said as he approached. A sly smile crossed his lips before he pulled her to him for a kiss. She gasped in surprise, although when she thought about it, she knew she shouldn't have been surprised at all. Some men would have been upset with her with how she'd handled things after the last serious discussion they'd had, but not Trey. Trey didn't have a vindictive bone in his body.

"Sorry," he said, breaking the kiss and clearing his throat. "You look so sexy in this formfitting teal dress, I had to do that before this night went any further. What were you saying?"

Kiara lightly shook her head out of its lustful state. "I was just saying that I'm glad you found me, and I wanted to say I'm so sorry for needing space this week."

"You don't have to apologize," Trey said. "There will always be a time in every relationship when one person may need a moment to evaluate some things. I knew I wasn't going anywhere—I just needed you to believe that."

"I believe it," Kiara said. "And I hope you know that I'm not going anywhere, either." Kiara stepped closer to Trey and placed her hands around his shoulders while his hands went around her waist. "Trey, my needing time to think had nothing to do with you and everything to do with me needing to face my own fears. I was so used to men claiming they love me, but not sticking around through the hard times, that I projected those fears onto our relationship. I was so surprised that you were so understanding, because what I told you is life-changing."

"I know," Trey said, brushing a piece of her hair out of her face. "But what you need to realize is that the biggest issue with what you told me was the fact that you had to endure that pain alone. I know that you are disappointed that you can't carry kids of your own, but, Kiara, if you want to be a mother, you can be a mother. There are so many children in the world who need a good family, and I happen to think that you and I would make amazing parents to some hopeful kids."

Kiara smiled as the backs of her eyelids burned with tears she was holding in. "Kids, as in plural? You'd be open to adoption?"

"Of course I would," Trey said, placing a light kiss on her forehead. "And yes, I mean plural. You never said so, but I have a feeling you always wanted more than one child. And although I never used to think I would be a good father, I feel differently now that I've spent so much time with my nephew. Being a family doesn't mean that you must be blood. It means loving one another unconditionally, and if we adopt, the children we adopt will be ours to love and raise."

Kiara leaned her head against Trey's chest. "How did I get so lucky to fall in love with a man as amazing as you are?"

Trey lifted her so he could stare into her eyes. "You love me?"

"Duh," she said with a laugh. She lifted her hand to his cheek. "Trey Moore, I love you more than words can say, and although I never saw you coming, I am so grateful that we found one another. I don't have any doubt in my heart that we'd make great parents to some amazing kids. Even though you said I don't have to apologize, I want to spend the rest of this week making sure you realize just how much I love you and how sorry I am."

"Is that why you rented me?" Trey asked. "To prove your love?"

Kiara nodded. "Yes. I figured a normal apology wouldn't do."

Trey glanced around his rooftop. "Did Carmen let you in?"

"She did," Kiara said. "I got her number from your friend Kendrick and told her that I needed her help. She was really sweet for doing this. She even helped further by giving your brother Max the second envelope so that he could give it to the security guard at Prescott George. I'm not a poet, but I'd hoped that the screenwriter in you would appreciate my efforts."

"I appreciate it," Trey said with a laugh. "But we'll work on your rhyming skills another time."

Kiara playfully hit Trey on the shoulder. "You're not cute."

"According to your second card, I'm sexy."

"I should have chosen a different word," she said, rolling her eyes.

Trey nodded. "Which is exactly why we'll practice your writing skills."

Kiara scrunched her forehead. "Is this to get me back for the time I came over to teach you how to care for your nephew? Because if it is, I hope you realize that this isn't the same thing."

"It's sort of the same thing," Trey said with a laugh. "Except, I know how to care for Matthew now."

Kiara shook her head, a smile spreading across her lips. "What am I going to do with you?"

"You mean, what are we going to do with each other?" Trey pulled her closer to him. "I can think of a few things."

Kiara squealed when Trey lifted her into his arms and carried her off the rooftop terrace and through the greenhouse. Her heartbeat quickened in anticipation, but it wasn't only for the intimate plans she saw formulating in Trey's mind. Her heart was racing in excitement as she thought about all the exciting things she and Trey had in their future. She wasn't ready to only make memories with the man who'd stolen her heart. She was ready to create the life and future she'd always dreamed of.

Epilogue

Two weeks later

"Trey, are you ready?"

Trey glanced inside the picnic basket once more to make sure he had everything he needed, before responding to Kiara. "Yes, I'm ready."

When Trey had asked Kiara if she wanted to take another impromptu weekend trip to the French Riviera, she hadn't hesitated to say yes. The past two weeks with Kiara had been just as beautiful as all their other times together, and he couldn't wait to see what their future held.

Trey's mother was back from her African safari and was eager to meet Kiara. Trey and Kiara had decided that they'd host a small pre-Thanksgiving dinner at their home so that their families could meet. It seemed that even though the families hadn't met yet, everyone was glad they'd found love in one another.

Trey was even slightly looking forward to celebrating Thanksgiving with Max, Derek and Reginald. They still weren't finished proving Reginald's innocence, or worse, confirming that he was guilty, but they were working on a few new leads that Trey hoped were promising.

"I'm so proud of you," Kiara said as they made their way to the beach. "I'm excited to go to my first awards show."

"I haven't even been nominated for an award yet," Trey said. He'd informed Kiara that his agents and producers were predicting that his latest screenplay was award worthy, and she'd taken what he'd said and run with it. Although he kept reminding her that there was no guarantee, he secretly appreciated how much faith she had in his work.

Another project that Trey was excited about was the fact that he'd convinced the LA board to allow Prescott George to team up with LA Little Ones for a mentorship program that focused more on children who were raised by a single parent. They planned on working on the preliminary programming and jump-starting that initiative in the New Year, after the holidays.

As they arrived on the beach, Trey was glad that it seemed to be deserted. There was a festival going on in town and he assumed people were there instead. Trey laid out their beach towels and took out the sandwiches, wine and fruit he'd packed.

"I've never had a picnic on the beach," Kiara said.

"Me, neither," Trey said. "I almost thought about setting up this picnic in the lifeguard stand."

Kiara laughed. "I'm not really in the mood to get caught again, so the beach is fine." They spent the next few minutes eating and talking about all the plans they needed to make for the holidays. It was a busy time for both of them, but Trey couldn't help thinking that this was going to be the best holidays he'd ever had, all because he'd found Kiara.

"Want to check out the water?" Trey asked.

"Sure." Kiara pulled off her maxi dress, revealing a white bikini.

"Damn," Trey said. "On second thought, do you want to head back to the villa and finally make love in the canopy bed?" Trey couldn't believe that, once again, they'd had sex everywhere but the canopy bed.

"No chance," Kiara said. "You're tempting, but this water has been calling my name since we arrived." Kiara ran into the ocean. Trey removed his T-shirt and raced toward her, splashing as much as he could. She squealed and splashed him back just as much.

"I was thinking," Trey said, pulling her to him as they stood knee-deep in the ocean. "You mentioned that you were okay with moving in with me and putting your house up for sale, but what if we keep your home for guests to stay in when they visit us from out of town? It's only a few blocks from my home, and we could always place it on Airbnb for the times we aren't using it."

Kiara smiled. "I think that's a fantastic idea."

"Great." Trey cleared his throat. "Because I was also

thinking that we could reach out to the adoption agency and get started on the paperwork. I know neither one of us wanted to wait too long to start a family, and the process could take a while."

Kiara frowned slightly. "I've heard it can take a while, too, but we aren't married yet, and I'm not sure how that will change the process."

"Then I guess we should change that." Trey smiled and kissed her lips softly before he reached into the pocket of his trunks and bent down on one knee. Kiara gasped as she covered her mouth with her hands.

"Kiara Woods, I fell for you the moment I laid eyes on you, and I've been falling ever since. There isn't a day that goes by that I don't realize how lucky I am to have you in my life. We may not be perfect, but together, I think we're as close to perfection as it gets. I hope that you realize that you will never have to go through any hardship on your own again because I will be there, right by your side. You are stronger than you realize. Powerful and wise beyond measure. And more beautiful than a woman has a right to be. Will you make me the happiest man on earth and marry me?"

Kiara wiped the tears that had fallen on her cheeks. "Yes, Trey. I'll marry you." Trey stood and placed the ring on her finger, the brilliant diamond catching the beautiful sunrays.

"I love you," Trey said, his voice filled with emotion.

"I love you, too." Kiara stood on tiptoes and placed her hand on the back of Trey's neck, pulling him in for a kiss. Trey enclosed his arms around Kiara and lifted her out of the water, spinning her in a circle, their lips never leaving from one another. It was a move that Trey had written in one of his romance screenplays, but never had he thought he'd be starring in his own love story with a leading lady as astounding as Kiara. She was his own romance heroine. She was his *everything*.

* * * * *

Get 4 FREE REWARDS!

We'll send you 2 FREE Books plus 2 FREE Mystery Gifts.

Harlequin® Desire books feature heroes who have it all: wealth, status, incredible good looks... everything but the right woman.

FREE
Value Over
$20